Temple Israel Library
Minneapolis, Minn.

———

RACHEL'S LEGACY

RACHEL'S LEGACY
HILA COLMAN

William Morrow and Company   New York   1978

Library of Congress Cataloging in Publication Data

Colman, Hila
   Rachel's legacy.

   Summary: Seven years after her mother dies, 17-year-old Ellie Levine learns her mother left a will, never executed, which could relieve the poverty existence of Ellie and her father during the Depression.
   [1. Jews in the United States—Fiction.   2. Inheritance and succession—Fiction.   3. Family life—Fiction]
I. Title.
PZ7.C7Rac   [Fic]   78-12783
ISBN 0-688-22154-8
ISBN 0-688-32154-2 lib. bdg.

Printed in the United States of America.
First Edition
1   2   3   4   5   6   7   8   9   10

While this book was inspired by some real events, the story as it appears in these pages bears little relation to what did happen. The characters are wholly the invention of the author, and any resemblance to particular persons is purely accidental.

*This book is dedicated
to the memory of my mother and father
and to their sisters and brothers,
who, in their early youth,
immigrated to this country.*

I am grateful to Leo Rosten for his book *Joys of Yiddish* (Pocket Books, N.Y.). I followed his spelling of Yiddish words and thereby avoided disagreement with dear friends who claimed to know better.

RACHEL'S LEGACY

Prologue

"You shouldn't work so hard," Ellie's father said sadly, shaking his head of bushy white hair. "It's not right. It's not the way you were brought up."

"Don't worry, Pop. It's all right. I don't mind. I'm fine." She pulled up the dusty carpet and swept the food crumbs and miscellaneous dirt out from under it. Expertly she worked by her father's heavy armchair, sweeping around it and beneath it, without asking him to move.

"Ach, your mother would tear her heart out to see you. For myself I don't care. I don't need anything anymore. Even my books I don't read. But you, a young girl, you should have dresses, good times, not be living this way." They were familiar words that Ellie had heard a hundred times. She had given up trying to argue with him, trying to tell him not to worry about her so much.

She didn't like to talk about what was happening. Words gave the facts substance, a reality she was not yet ready to face. In the beginning, when she and her father had first moved to the shabby, run-down hotel, Ellie had thought it somewhat of a lark. Lying wide awake on the lumpy sofa bed in the sitting room, with her father next door in the tiny hall bedroom, she had listened to arguments, crying, sometimes screams coming from the street and the lobby, too, and thought she might have been in the middle of a movie thriller.

Never before had she come close to people like those she passed in the hotel lobby—seedy men with vacant eyes and unshaven faces, old women carrying bundles picked out of garbage pails.

Ellie had felt both fascination and pity. They were people out of another world, a world from which she had been carefully protected. But she didn't walk past them with unseeing eyes. She made friends. She got to know Mrs. O'Carney and Mr. Schiff, and the son who sometimes came to visit old Mr. Kavasch. She knew most of their names and their family stories. But up until now she hadn't felt *of* them. She had still felt protected, safe.

Being poor, she kept telling herself, was for her temporary, a novelty, an interesting experience that would do her good. To have to look for a job because they needed the money would strengthen her character. Secretly she even took some pleasure out of the fact that now she was one of the masses, one of the millions of unemployed. She felt an empathy with the people around her, with the long breadlines, the men who marched on Washington, a kinship she had not felt as rich Ellie Levine.

Not long ago, the previous June, in fact, a job had been the furthest thing from Ellie's mind. She had come home from her freshman year at a small, expensive women's college looking forward to the usual summer in the big country house on Long Island. There she went swimming, played tennis, went horseback riding, and danced at the country club. Sometimes she could wheedle the chauffeur, Roger, to let her drive the big Cadillac with the top down and

Fanny the cook to make her favorite pastry. Every morning she awoke to the wonderful smells of fresh biscuits and roses and the sea outside her window.

But last June, when she arrived home with her usual bounce, her father had greeted her with tears in his eyes. He hadn't had the heart to tell her while she was at school, and anyway, he said, her tuition and board had been paid. "The house is sold," he told her. "I needed the money, although those *gonifs,* those thieves, gave me *bubkes.* Like a knife in my heart to take their money, but beggars can't be choosers." The tears had rolled down his cheeks. "I'm no good. You should find yourself a good husband to take care of you. I'm finished. I should be in the grave next to your mother. An old man with no money is better off dead; he shouldn't take up space. The world already is too crowded."

Little by little the story came out. Her father had weathered the stock market crash of 1929 without losing much because he had not been playing the market. Instead he had put his money into real estate, but now, as the Depression had stretched out, his tenants couldn't pay their rent, and he couldn't pay his mortgages. Finally the banks had foreclosed, and he lost his buildings. He was vague with Ellie about what was left but insisted that they could live for a couple of years on his savings and a tiny income from some bonds if they were very careful.

Ellie had been stunned, but quite cheerfully, without telling her father, she had sold one of her mother's diamond brooches. She told her father she had money left over from her clothes allowance. During the summer, in the drenching city heat, she had taken the subway every morning to a school for a crash four-week course in shorthand and typing. Their sign read, *We guarantee you a job.* Being a secretary, she thought, would be interesting. The employment agencies said that even if you started in a typing pool, you could get promoted quickly if you were smart. But there had been no start. There were no jobs.

In October, when their lease was up, she and her father had moved out of their large, sunlit New York apartment into the two tiny, dark rooms in a building on a West Side street that called itself a hotel but was little more than a rooming house for others as poor as themselves. Mostly they were old people who shuffled in and out of the lobby clutching their brown paper bags of meager meals.

Now, in the cold midwinter, after many days of no heat and no hot water in the dingy hotel, Ellie was beginning to come out from the protective blanket she had wrapped herself in. The reality of roaches, poor meals, and her father's drawn, gloomy face every time he had to go to the savings bank to make another withdrawal was making itself felt. She could no longer delude herself that she was different. That because she was young, reasonably attractive, and with a good education and background, she could say at will she had had enough. Good-bye, all you hardy, brave souls. I admire you all, but I'm going back to my comfortable, happy world. Forgive me, but I'm not helping you any by hanging around. . . .

Finally she was really feeling the shock. She wasn't different. Papa couldn't save them; Mama wasn't alive. It was hard to believe that everything was gone—the house, the parties, the expensive clothes, the wasted food. Eventually they might even starve, as lots of other people were doing. Ellie's illusions were quickly fading. Being poor was no joke. It was real and it might be forever.

When Ellie finished her cleaning, she washed her face, put on her ten-cent-store make-up, a woolen hat (black to go with everything), and the winter coat she had almost outgrown.

She kissed her father good-bye and stepped out of the darkness of the dank lobby into a gray New York February afternoon. It wasn't much brighter outside than in, but the fresh air was a relief after the continual stale smells of the illegal cooking on the one-burner stoves the tenants kept in their tiny rooms. "Like living in a cell," her father often said, hunching up his body when he spoke, as if to breathe would use up all the air in the room.

Ellie hadn't told him where she was going. "Just for a walk," she said, and he had given her his sad, knowing smile and a nod of his head. He had stopped asking weeks ago, "So, *nu,* what happened today?" He knew what happened. There were no jobs.

Out on the street Ellie could see the shanties on Riverside Drive where some of the unemployed were living, boxes made of anything the men could find to put a roof over their families. The shacks were illegal, but no one tried to get the squatters out. The year of 1932 had opened with fourteen million people out of work, but President Hoover did not believe that the Federal Government should interfere to give relief in this depression.

But that February day Ellie felt her luck was turning. She felt optimistic. It was nothing more than a feeling, but as the realities of her life became more and more discouraging, Ellie was learning to lean on her hunches and instincts.

She was headed for Child's Restaurant on Columbus Circle where she'd heard there might be a job for a waitress. It would be odd working there because that was where, when Ellie used to go dancing at the Biltmore or went to the theater or a late movie, she and her friends ended up for pancakes. She remembered feeling sorry for the waitresses, having to work so late and carrying their loaded trays to tables crowded with hilarious, zany kids who didn't care what a mess they left. Yet now, if she could only be one of those waitresses, she'd be the happiest girl in the world.

But before she went there she had better take care of the document she had stuck in her pocketbook. She had hardly read it, a legal document with a lot of boring legal language. It had arrived in the morning mail, with a brief note from her cousin Sadie's lawyer asking her to sign it before a notary public and send it back to him. There was a stamped, addressed envelope, for which Ellie was grateful as the post office was long blocks away on Amsterdam Avenue and she had no stamps. Such things cheered her, like the butcher throwing in extra bones for soup, or the old woman on the corner giving her a bunch of flowers at the end of the day when she was ready to go home. Ellie looked upon these small events as signs that she had not been singled out for a life of ill fortune.

The stationery store was dark and untidy, and at first she did not see old Mr. Rabinowitz behind the piles of newspapers, paper pads, and glass cases of penny candy. But his voice called out to her, "Good morning, young lady. You want your father's paper?"

"I'll pick it up on my way home. I need something notarized. You can do it, can't you?"

"Yes, yes. For you I do it special. I charge you only fifty cents. A bargain."

Ellie laughed. "And anyone else a quarter. Here. Do I have to sign it first?" She laid the paper out on the counter.

"Did you read what you are signing?"

Ellie shook her head. "It's from my cousin Sadie's lawyer, something about her husband's estate. He was my real cousin. She's just a cousin by marriage."

"I know who your cousin Nathan Solomon was. A fine young man. A rich man, he died a rich man. Too young to die. Let me look at this paper before you sign it."

"All right, but I don't have much time. Do you have to look at it all?" she asked, as she watched him reading all the fine print slowly and carefully.

Mr. Rabinowitz nodded his head. "Don't be in such a hurry. Did your father read this?"

"No. I forgot to tell him about it. It's just a form, isn't it? Some legal red tape?"

Mr. Rabinowitz finished reading the entire document before he answered her. Then he put the paper on the table and looked at her with his pale-blue eyes. "I'm not going to notarize this for you. You're signing away a fortune, young lady. You show this to your father and take it to a lawyer. This is no good for you."

Ellie stared at him as if he might have gone crazy. "What are you talking about? What fortune?"

Mr. Rabinowitz pointed to the legal sheet. "You read this. They want you should sign a release so that Nathan Solomon's estate shouldn't be responsible for the money coming to you from your mother's will. You ever get any money from your mother's will? I say you didn't. I don't know what went on, but something fishy. It don't smell good. There's money coming to you, or such a smart lawyer wouldn't take so much trouble. I don't sign nothing. Take my advice and go to a lawyer."

"My own family's not going to gyp me," Ellie said indignantly.

"Your cousin by marriage," Mr. Rabinowitz said gently. "You said yourself."

Ellie picked up the document gingerly. She read it hurriedly. It *was* a release. "You're a very kind man," she said, raising her eyes to Mr. Rabinowitz's gray face. "Someone else would have just notarized it."

"Not me. I read first. A millionaire I'm not, but I'm not so stupid either. I know what's right."

Outside, Ellie headed back toward West End Avenue. She forgot about going for the waitress job. Her head was in the clouds. She didn't understand what she was being asked to release, but Mr. Rabinowitz had said a fortune. . . . Her parents had been well off, she knew that much, and she had never questioned where the money had gone to when several years earlier her father and her uncle Iz, Nathan Solomon's father, had dissolved their partnership and their business of manufacturing children's dresses. Had all of her father's share gone into buying those apartment houses in the Bronx that he had recently lost? And what about her mother's will? She had never even heard of a will when her mother died seven years ago, when Ellie was ten.

Ellie rushed home with all these questions and more crowding her mind. She found her father sitting where she had left him, yesterday's newspapers, the *New York Herald Tribune* and the *Jewish Daily Forward,* his two extravagances, lying on the table beside him. He was dressed as if still going to business, his white, starched collar immaculate, his tie neat, his gold watch and chain in place across his buttoned vest, his black shoes polished (a job he took pride in—"just as good as the shoeshine boy used to do").

Ellie gave him the document to read and then told him what Mr. Rabinowitz had said. "What about Mama's will? I never knew she had a will or left me anything."

Her father kept looking at the paper in his hand. "Nathan had a good lawyer," he muttered. "He left a big estate. Your cousin made good money and had a rich wife besides. But to die such a young man. Diabetes—they call it the Jewish disease. A good thing his mother died before him, your aunt Esther. The old men are left, your uncle Iz and me. . . ."

Ellie could see he was upset and his mind was going back. "You're not so old, Pop," she said soothingly. She waited a few minutes before she asked him again, softly, about her mother's will.

"Yes, she left a will. Your mother was a smart business-woman. She had everything taken care of, and she was right. I'm the *shlemiel.* I should have done what she said, but it didn't seem to make sense." He threw up his hands with a gesture of despair. "I was still not such an old man when she died, and you were a child. She said in her will I should sell out my share of the business and put the money in trust for me and for you, set up a trust fund like Sam Rosenwald did for his children, and we'd never have to worry again. But your cousin Nathan, an educated lawyer and executor of the will with me, we talked it over, and we said, 'What for? Why sell out a good business?' And what would I do, sit home and twiddle my thumbs? We didn't do anything. The will is still lying in the safety box."

Her father stood up and there were tears in his eyes. "You should sue the estate, you should sue me. We were criminals, Nathan and me. He's dead but his money is here. I've got nothing, but I can go to jail. I don't mind, I deserve it. I lost it all. Your mother was smart. She knew what a *shlemiel* I am, but I didn't listen to her. I should be punished. You got a right, Ellie, you got a right to the money, it should belong to you. . . ."

Her father was excited and crying, and she tried to quiet him down. "Take it easy, Pop. Don't get yourself all upset. The money isn't here. The money from the business is gone, isn't it?"

Mr. Levine nodded his head. "All gone." He raised his eyes to hers. "But I'm here, I should pay, and Nathan's money is good for it. Don't you understand? His estate is responsible. That's why they want you to sign, so they shouldn't be. But you see. You sue them and me. Mr. Rabinowitz is right."

"But what if you went to jail?"

"Do I care? I think how your mother worked all her life since she was a child. I can hear her telling me all the hardships she had, she and her sisters and their mother. There was no finer woman in the world than your mother, every day I mourn for her. Your cousin Sadie has so much money she wouldn't miss it."

"I couldn't sue you, Pop. Never. I couldn't do it."

"Don't be so finicky. You could finish going to college. Your mother always dreamed you should be a lawyer like your cousin Nathan. Over and over again she said, 'I want Ellie to be a lawyer.' She worked night and day that you should have a fine education, that you shouldn't have to worry. Every day I can hear her voice talking to me. . . . At least talk to a lawyer. I'll call up Mr. Weinstein, a *landsman* from my society. He won't charge me nothing."

"Are you sure?"

Her father shrugged. "Who knows these days? Everybody out for himself. What can he charge? I got nothing. I'm a broken man, Ellie. For me nothing matters. For your mother's sake, for you, I'd give my life. What happens to me has no importance. Every day I hear your mother's voice telling me her story. . . ."

"Yes, Pop, I know." She too had heard bits and pieces all her life, but never anything about a will. She would take it out of the vault in the bank and try to put the pieces together so that she could decide what to do. The hard-earned money her mother had worked for. . . . For executors to disregard a will must be a criminal offense. . . .

It was not going to be an easy decision.

Ellie sat beside her father and held his hand, patting

it gently. He *was* a broken man, and she wished this piece of news had not come to torment him further. He had aged ten, twenty years since her mother died. If she could get Cousin Nathan's estate to give her some of the money without hurting her father, she could get him out of this dreary, depressing room where he sat most of every day brooding. . . .

Yet somewhere inside of her there was a perplexing feeling that she did not want the money. Her reaction was almost one of resentment. She had been too young when her mother died to understand her feelings then. But now suddenly she felt that her mother was still trying to control her life, even from the grave. Her mother had always seemed to use, undoubtedly without meaning to or realizing it, the comforts that money could buy to make up for her consuming absorption in the business, to atone for the series of nursemaids hired to replace the homey mother for whom Ellie had longed. Mothers like her friends had. Part of Ellie felt that the money now would rob her of her chance—a chance to do she did not know what, unless it was to prove to herself that money wasn't as important as her mother, working herself to an early death to make it, had thought it was.

And for what? The horror of what had happened hit Ellie like a physical blow. All the hard work, the money gone down the drain. Ellie remembered her mother coming home from work so tired she could hardly stand, her face white and drawn. And her resentment washed away. She had been too young to understand her mother—her knowledge of her was based on stories she had been told by her father and her aunts

—and now anger, not against her mother but *for* her, took over. It was as if her life had been thrown away. Ellie could not blame her father, he thought he was acting for the best, but Cousin Nathan had known the law, and still he had let this outrageous loss take place. Nathan, whom her mother had adored so much, was the one who had betrayed her trust. And that silly rich wife of his. . . . Let her live in this awful place and see how she liked it. In her fancy Park Avenue apartment, she should be ashamed that her husband's uncle and cousin lived in such squalor. Ellie felt herself boiling with rage and frustration. She had better take a few days to calm down before she went to see Nathan's widow.

"I'd better go buy some food," Ellie said. "What do you want?" Her question was rhetorical since there was not much that could be cooked on their one-burner nor much that they could afford.

But her father didn't answer. His eyes had the far-away look she knew so well, a sign that his mind had gone back. He was turning over again the early days, remembering his Rachel, her mother, and the endless stories she had told of how she had come to America, the good things and the bad, and he was remembering their courtship and their days together. Whenever her mother had started, "Like it was yesterday, I remember. In 1908 we left the old country, Mama, my sisters and me," Ellie knew a story was coming. . . .

1

Like sardines we were packed on the boat. Mama said it was a good thing they didn't give us much to eat, because if anyone gained an ounce no one could move. There was not much we could eat anyway, all the food was *trayf*, so we had only black bread and butter and herring and water. For sixteen days. It was a terrible time.

When Papa had died, Mama sold the store he had in our village and packed up our things to go to America. The streets were paved with gold, she said. All our clothes were in one trunk, with Papa's prayer shawl, and she made a separate bundle of her pots and dishes and her long brown hair she had saved all these years from the time her head had been shaved before her wedding. How I hated that hair. Mama called it a rat and believe me that is what it looked like. I was afraid to touch it. I was only twelve years old, but I made up my mind then I would never wear a *shaytl*, a wig like Mama's, even if it meant I'd never get married. I didn't tell Mama my vow.

Mama thought we had a room on the boat with four berths, one for her, one for little eight-year-old Ida, one for me, Rachel, and one for fifteen-year-old Esther. But when we got there we discovered already another family, and it was so crowded that we three girls slept out on the deck with the other people. On the deck was more air, but it wasn't good air because everyone was sick, Mama and my two sisters, too. Everyone except me, although the smell was terrible.

Mama was afraid. I didn't know how many fears Mama had until we left home. Fear it was that made her leave in the first place. Nothing else in the world would have driven her from our village, from our house, a house she had gone to as a bride and where her three girls were born. She was afraid of the Cossacks, afraid of the pogroms, afraid the children would starve. She was afraid she'd be forced to take another husband (a widow was only to be pitied in that village) and for Mama there had been only one man in her life, her beloved Nathan. On the boat she was more afraid. She kept her money tied up inside her corset cover, and Mama, who used to bathe herself and all of us every Friday for the Sabbath, didn't take her clothes off once during the whole sixteen days.

"If we have to go in the lifeboats," she said, "I want to be dressed." She was afraid of drowning, afraid of the food, afraid of the people.

Me, I was the opposite. Not like my sisters, Esther and little Ida, who clung to her skirts. I became more venturesome. I wanted to be with the people; I wanted to watch the waves. Hungrily I watched the others eat food we weren't allowed. I ran around the ship like a puppy sticking my nose into everything while Mama and my sisters huddled together sick and scared.

I brought back to Mama little pieces of news I picked up: the lady with the braids around her head was going to meet her husband she hadn't seen in five years; the pretty young girl was going to America to marry a man she never met. She was showing his picture to everyone, and he had fine mustaches but a wart on his nose. The rabbi's wife was going to have a baby. I saw everything and heard everything.

Friday nights were beautiful. I'll never forget the first one. By some miracle there was no rocking, and although Mama cried because they wouldn't let her light her candles, a rabbi on board said the Shabbes prayers, and the women sat quietly while the men stood *davening* in whispers. Later the moon came out, and someone began a song, and then everyone was singing and it was beautiful. I wanted to cry.

One old woman was very kind to Mama when she and the girls were sick. She gave them medicine; it didn't do much good but Mama said that to have someone take the trouble made her feel better. The old woman asked if I was happy to go to America.

"I think so," I told her. I didn't tell her I was a little scared too. I didn't know what to expect. Mama's cousin Sam had written saying how wonderful America was, but when she wrote to tell him that we were coming, his next letter said that she shouldn't expect to pick up gold from the street. There were some people on the boat who spoke English, and it sounded so funny to me I was afraid I'd never learn it.

"You don't have to speak English," the old woman said. "My son wrote me that where the Jews live, Yiddish is good enough. A new language I don't have to learn at my age."

But I wanted to learn. On the boat I learned to count up to ten: one, two, three, four, five, six, seven, eight, nine, ten. And a few words I learned. I taught them to Esther and Ida, who were too shy to speak.

Mama didn't like I was in such a hurry to become American. "Don't forget who you are," she said to me on the boat. She said the same thing many, many times, like if she could, she'd drill a hole in my head and put the words inside. Some things I wanted to forget. Not our village, where I was born and everyone knew everyone else, where in the summertime I could pick flowers. Farmers came to Papa's store with their horses and carts, and Papa was an important, educated man, a trustee of the Houses of Study and a member of the Community Council. He wasn't a nobody and was proud of us girls the same as if we were sons.

What I never wanted to think about was when the whole village boarded itself up, when it was said the Russian soldiers were coming to take the boys and men into the Army and to do harm to the women and girls. No one went out on the street, even to go to the toilet was a fearful journey, and for days we had nothing to eat but *krupnik*, a barley-and-potato soup Mama cooked. Thank God the soldier's didn't come, but two, three times, I don't remember, we had to hide because we thought they were coming. Mama said such a fear hanging over his head killed Papa, although the doctor said he died of the lung sickness. But maybe Mama knew better.

One day there was great excitement on the boat—we saw land. The deck already was jammed, but more people came out, people hidden away the whole trip. Some were crying from joy, and there was cheering and waving although there was no one to wave to. Everyone was telling everyone else, "Look, look," as if one had to show another. I was so excited I thought I'd wet my pants. America. A country where there'd be no Russian soldiers, where everyone was rich, where Cousin Sam lived in a house where you didn't have to go outside to do your duty. It was going to be like stepping into heaven. Ida was jumping up and down from excitement, and Mama and Esther both had looks on their faces like they were seeing the Messiah.

Out of the mist and the clouds, there suddenly came a huge statue, a beautiful lady with a crown on her head, her arm out, holding high up in the air a torch. The Statue of Liberty. She was like a queen, and for no reason she made me cry. I felt she knew that Mama and Esther and Ida and me were on the ship and we were scared and she would take care of us. I'd be a tiny speck next to her, she was so big, but I felt I wanted to put my arms around her and tell her how beautiful she was and that I was going to try to be very good. In America I was not going to forget to feed the chickens and I would be careful not to dirty my clean clothes in the mud.

"Wash your faces, brush your hair." Mama nervously was giving out orders while she was gathering together all our belongings to be pushed back into the trunk. We all had to sit on it to make it close. Where we were going to land was called Castle Garden—a name when we heard it in Yiddish made us quiver with hope and excitement.

"Are we going to live in a castle?" little Ida asked.

"I don't think so," Mama told her.

"But we'll have a garden," Esther said.

"I'm going to grow roses." That had been a dream of mine since I had once gone with Papa to visit a man who lived in a big house where I had been told to play in the garden. All kinds of flowers grew in the garden, but there had been a wall with a little door in it, and I'd opened the door and there on the other side of the wall was another garden with nothing but roses in it. Hundreds of roses: red, white, and pink. You can't imagine how many roses. First I closed my eyes so I could just smell them all, and then I flitted around like a bee from one bush to another until I couldn't stand it anymore. I picked one and stuck it inside my dress. I kept it in my dress all day, and when I got home I put it under the pillow on my bed. Later I put it in a book, and then I guess I forgot about it because I never saw it again.

Castle Garden. Their heads should grow like turnips in the ground to call such a place Castle Garden. An old stone building and a courtyard filled with people who couldn't get into the building. Mama was excited like crazy. "Cousin Sam, he was to meet us, to take us to his house. How can you find anyone in such a place?"

Jews, Gentiles, we were all together. Next to me was standing a little girl, Eileen I heard later her name was. A Gentile, and she was crying. "What's the matter?" I asked her. But she couldn't understand me, and she kept on crying. Her mother tried to comfort her. She took her in her arms and said soft words to her. Eileen had a bird in a cage. I found out she was crying because they were going to take the bird away from her. They said she couldn't bring a bird into America. I wondered, What kind of a country is this where you can't bring a bird?

Some people found their relatives, but we slept outside crowded like animals, like we were still on the boat. Someone brought bread and sausage, but Mama said we could eat only the bread because the sausage wasn't kosher. The next day most of the Gentiles left, my friend Eileen too, and the Jews who had a place to go, but we had to stay. And the worst was yet to come. We were examined for our health, and they found that Ida had nits in her hair. We were all so ashamed, but Mama told them Ida got them on the boat. Ida yelled her head off when they washed her hair with a black soap. I was ashamed for her but I felt sorry, too, so I gave her a piece of candy a lady had given to me.

The whole day Mama kept looking for Cousin Sam. In the afternoon she cried because she didn't know what to do. "We should go home," Esther said. "I don't like America."

"We can't go home. I sold everything. There is no home. And I spent a lot of our money for our fare. *Oy vay iz mir*! My poor children, what shall we do?"

Ida was clinging to Mama's skirt, and even Esther, the oldest, was crying. But I didn't want to go home. We were here, and terrible as it was, I wanted to see America. Here, it was said, there was room enough for everyone, and Jews didn't have to be afraid. There were no pogroms, no Cossacks. I had a vision of a beautiful life, a beautiful country on the other side of the wall from Castle Garden. And somehow we had to get to it.

The next day Cousin Sam came. "Such a mix-up. I got the wrong information, stupid people. . . ." He didn't apologize; he was just angry.

"It's all right. When you don't speak the language, it's hard," Mama said.

Cousin Sam exploded. "Who says I don't speak English? I speak it fine, like I was born here." He shook his finger under Mama's nose. "In my house no Yiddish. We speak American, that's all."

"I hope not in my house," Mama said softly. "I hope in my house we don't forget who we are."

Cousin Sam carried our things to a wooden cart. There was no horse, so he pushed the cart himself through the streets. The day was hot and the sweat poured down his face and his beard. I didn't remember Cousin Sam very well with his thick, dark hair and his red beard. He was almost like a stranger to me. He had a strong body but pushing the cart over the bumpy cobblestone streets seemed to be hard. Everything was new and strange, and after many streets it was a relief to get to where the Jews lived. A relief to hear our own language, to see the bearded fathers with their *yarmulkahs* and the women and children with familiar faces.

The houses didn't look like anything I had ever seen before. They were packed one on top of the other and rose five, six stories high so that hardly any sun came down to the narrow streets. You had to walk one by one around the pushcarts. Everything you'd ever want was set out for sale. Everything they said about America was true. Such riches. Pots and pans, dresses, pants, shoes, vegetables, fruit, chickens, meats, sausages—there was nothing you couldn't buy. For so much there had to be a lot of customers.

Cousin Sam stopped in front of one of the houses. It looked the same as the others. Five stories high with an iron stairway on the outside. Cousin Sam said that it was the fire escape, but God forbid there should be a fire, how would the people get out? Each landing was filled with clothes hanging, plants, babies in baskets, all kinds of rubbish. Such narrow steps you could fall and break your neck.

Sam took our trunk and bags from the cart, and each of us carried something inside. I wanted to get out the minute I got in. Such a smell. The barnyard at home was sweet compared to this. At least that smelled healthy, like something from nature, but this—like rotten eggs, something unclean that would never go away because no one would dare to touch it.

Four flights of stairs we climbed, Cousin Sam with the trunk on his back. At last, when he opened the door to his apartment, it smelled better, the smell of a good soup cooking on the stove.

Lena, his wife, was genuinely happy to see us. A real welcome she gave us—we should sit down, we should take off our shoes, a cup of coffee would cheer us up, maybe a piece of crumb cake, too. Her children stared at us while we ate. Saul, her oldest, looked at Esther like a man looks at a woman, but maybe he decided she was too young or too much of a greenhorn. In a few minutes he went to a corner to read a book. His mother said he had already had his bar mitzvah, but he was still going to Hebrew school anyway. "A real *yeshiva bucher*," she called him. There was also a little girl about Ida's age called Rose.

I was happy there were other children, but friendly they weren't, and they talked to each other in English. Like Cousin Sam said, they didn't speak Yiddish in his house. Mama couldn't understand a word, and the girls and me maybe a word here and there. Only when Cousin Sam and Lena spoke to us in Yiddish did we know what they were saying.

"In no time the children will learn English," Cousin Lena said. (Cousin by marriage she was.) "And you'll learn too," she said to Mama.

"Maybe," Mama said quietly.

"In America you'll speak English." Cousin Sam twirled his mustache and bit hard into a red apple. In two minutes he ate up the apple and then cleaned his teeth with a toothpick. He kept the toothpick in his mouth, chewing on it as if it tasted very good.

I wondered where we were going to sleep. The sun was going down, and I was tired. So much furniture they had. A sewing machine next to the stove, a sofa, chairs, a big round table, everything in the room where they cooked and ate. I hoped we didn't have to sleep there, too. Fortunately, there was another little room with a big bed, and we three girls got into it. But first we had to move a pile of boys' knee pants. What did Saul need so many pants for? I wondered. But I didn't wonder for long. I fell asleep right away to the sound of Mama and Cousin Sam and Lena talking in the next room. My first night in America.

2

Esther was the eldest, but she was the most timid. She was worse than Mama, afraid to go out on the street, afraid of the horses, afraid of the people, afraid of her own shadow. But I liked the noise, the women and children, the men calling out, "Old clothes, old clothes for sale," or "Fresh vegetables, buy my fresh vegetables. . . ." I wanted to be out on the street, out of the hot, stifling apartment where if there was a drop of air, there were too many people to breathe it.

How can I explain to you what it was like to be here? Every day something new to find, a new word to learn, a new sight to see. Always on the street there would be some excitement: if a horse stumbled and fell, a crowd would gather around to watch; if two boys had a fight, you'd think the circus had come; if a pushcart tipped over, everyone would see who could pick up the most onions, potatoes, whatever there was, like they were pieces of gold. I didn't know from being rich or poor then. I didn't know from fine carriages and fancy clothes, from restaurants, shows, nothing. Later, much later I learned about diamonds and silk dresses, about the opera house—*oy*, how I loved to get dressed up and listen to the music—but then if Mama gave me a sausage sandwich and a new pickle I was in heaven. If I walked five blocks to a little park and felt the sun, it was beautiful. In Cousin Sam's apartment there was never no sun.

Sure we were poor. Poor like I hope my children will

never know. But we were no different from everyone around us. On Delancey Street there were no rich people, and outside of that what did I know? Maybe four, five blocks, that's all.

But those blocks I knew, and I knew best of all the walk from our house to the factory to get the knee pants. Those pants I saw piled up on the bed that first night weren't Saul's. They were Work. Lena sewed them on the machine, and right away she showed Mama and Esther how to make the buttonholes and to sew on the buttons. My job was to carry the bundles back and forth from the house to the factory. Sometimes Ida and Rose came with me. Saul never. He was busy with his books. How I hated him and his books. Big bundles, heavy like bricks, I carried. Cousin Sam was the cutter at the factory, and though he was not what I'd call a kind man, he tried not to make the bundles too big for my skinny arms. But the office lady would say, "Here, I got another dozen. Let her take them. We got to get the order out."

Whenever I had an extra-heavy bundle to carry, I'd think of that Saul, sitting home catching the only breeze there was out on the fire escape, eating his bread heavy with *shmaltz*. Always he was stuffing his mouth with bread and chicken fat—reading his books. So many books I thought should make him smart like a professor, but he didn't know even to say thank you when you gave him his bread.

We were living at Cousin Sam's maybe a month, maybe two, I don't know, I guess two since it was beginning to turn chilly, when I got up my nerve and said one evening. "Why can't Saul carry the bundles sometimes?"

His mother looked like she was going to faint. Then she drew herself up tall. "Saul? Saul has to study. Already he is the smartest boy in the school. The rabbi says he will go to the American school and be a lawyer. It's not for Saul to carry bundles."

Saul looked at me and smirked, and I could have smashed his fat face in. How I hated him. To tell the truth, I didn't like any of them except little Rose. She wasn't old enough to be stuck-up.

I knew Mama was saving some money. I'd seen a jar where she'd put a few pennies in when she could, once in a while even a dollar bill. "Is it for us to have our own apartment?" I asked. The three of us were sleeping in one bed, Mama was sleeping on a blanket on the floor—she said it was good for her back, tired from the sewing all day—and we were having to pay Cousin Sam for the privilege. It wasn't a home.

Mama nodded her head and whispered, "I'm saving what I can, but it's going to take a long time."

What could I do to make more money? How could we get out of there to live by ourselves? My head was troubled with such thoughts. After that the bundles couldn't be big enough for me. When I went to the factory, I asked, "Haven't you got more? Give me more." I'd carry so much my arms would feel like they would drop off before I got home.

Then one day I came home with my arms full and found Mama crying her eyes out. I looked around quick to see if Esther and Ida were alive, and they were crouching in a corner like scared rabbits.

Cousin Lena was wailing with Mama. "*Oy vay*, such a foolish woman." She turned to mama and screamed, "Couldn't you wait till I came home? You had to be in such a hurry to give away your money? You couldn't tell him to come back again?"

"How would I know? A fine Jewish man, a religious man who kissed the *mezuzah*. Should I know he was a *gonif*? Should I know one Jew would steal from another, would steal from a poor widow and children?"

Lena shook her head in despair. "You think every Jew is honest? Such a stupid woman I never heard. . . ."

"What happened?" I asked. My heart was sinking. I was afraid to look at Mama's jar with the money. I knew it would be empty.

"Tell her. Tell her what you did," Lena ordered Mama.

"I thought I was doing the right thing," Mama said, sobbing. "How should I know? In the old country you could trust people."

"What happened?" I yelled.

"Is it wrong to think we could make more money?" Mama asked between sobs. "A peddler came and said he had a fine sewing machine he could sell me. Like new. Such a bargain. I could sew pants like Lena, and the money would grow fast. So I gave him half the money. We agreed he should bring the machine, and I'd give him the other half. But he never came back." She looked up, hopeful. "Maybe he had an accident. Maybe he'll still come."

"You'll never see him again," Lena said cruelly. "It's a wonder you didn't give him all the money. A foolish woman. . . ."

"At least you still have half," I said to Mama to comfort her. But my heart was heavy with sadness. Who knew now when we could ever move?

And that wasn't all our trouble. It seemed God had

decided for us to survive in America should not be easy. What have we done, I thought, to have so much hardship?

A few weeks after the money was gone, I was getting ready to carry a bundle of knee pants to Cousin Sam in the factory. First I went out in the back to the toilet. (Our dream had not been fulfilled. We had no inside toilet where Sam and Lena lived.) When I came in, there was an uproar in the apartment so loud I thought maybe someone was dead. Mama and Lena were screaming at each other. The girls were crying, and that fat no-good Saul looked scared. This time I didn't have to ask. I could see for myself.

The bundle of pants was a pile of wet rags. The stupid lummox Saul had spilled a pot of tea on them. It was no laughing matter. I wouldn't dignify him with a word. I shook out the pants and rolled them in a towel, but it was a waste of time. They were like washed in mud.

When everyone quieted down, Mama asked tearfully, "What are we going to do? We are finished." She looked at Saul with hate in her eyes, but that clumsy fool had nothing to say.

"Let him take them back," I said. "Let him tell them what happened."

"He won't know what to say. He'll only make it worse." For once his mother spoke the truth. "You better go, Rachel. You explain to Sam. He'll tell the boss." She stopped and looked at Saul and then at me. "Don't tell Sam that Saul did it. Just say it was an accident. If you must say something, say that I did it."

Mama was shocked. "You would lie to your own husband! Better he should know what kind of a son he has."

"Saul's a good boy," his mother said. "It wasn't his fault, but his father has a temper. Please, I know what I'm doing."

While they were talking I was thinking about what I was going to say. From the beginning I knew I'd be the one elected. In a way it made me proud. Young as I was, I was the one Mama and my sisters depended on more and more in America. Mama stayed in the house most of the time working on the pants, and besides she was afraid of the streets. By now Esther liked to go out, but she never wanted to go alone and nagged me to go with her. So together we did the shopping from the push-carts, but never would she make up her mind. I had to choose cauliflower or potatoes, chicken or pot roast. It was always "Rachel, you decide." And with little Ida, it was "Give me a penny for candy," or "Button up my shoes," like I was the mama. Ida was smart, and already she was almost speaking English like she was born here. Mama didn't like it when she talked so much in English, because Mama couldn't understand and wasn't in a hurry to learn, so she was many times scolding Ida. I worried about Ida picking up American ways too fast, bad talk from the streets, but like Mama I too was proud she was so smart.

But I wasn't worrying about Ida with those pants in front of me. I had to figure out what to do. I was scared. Scared to take them to Sam the way they looked, and scared to throw them away and not take them. Those pants stood between us and starvation.

"Let's try one and see if we can get out the stain," Lena said. We scrubbed and scrubbed until I thought we'd make a hole right through the material. But nothing happened. The pants looked the same when we finished as when we began. Terrible. So I said I might as well go and get it over with, but believe me, inside I was shivering.

With the bundle in my arms I walked slowly to the factory.

"Cousin Sam," I said, "we had an accident." I spoke before he had a chance to look at the pants.

"What happened? Someone get hurt? Don't stand there like a fool. Tell me."

"No one got hurt. Just the pants. A pot of tea got spilled."

Sam tore the bundle apart, and his face turned red with rage. "A pot of tea! A bucket of tea. *Oy vay*. What *shlemiel* could do such a thing?" He wrung his hands and then grabbed my blouse. "Tell me, who did this?"

"What difference does it make who did it? It's done. What will happen?" I asked nervously.

"You'll have to pay for the pants. That's what will happen. Two dozen good pants! You think Mr. Cohen can afford to throw away two dozen pants? Tell me, who did it?"

I looked him straight in the eyes. "I don't know. I came home and it was done."

"You're lying to me. You did it. You think you can fool around with Sam Finklestein, you're wrong. I do everything for you like you were my own daughter. I take four of you into my house, I give you food, I give you work, and what thanks do I get? You lie, you ruin the pants, *oy vay iz mir*. I'll have a heart attack yet."

Mr. Cohen, the boss, came into the front room where we were standing. "Don't have a heart attack, Sam. What's going on here?"

Sam showed him the pants. "An accident. But don't worry, we'll make it up. She'll make it up. She'll work hard until the pants are paid off. It'll be all right." His voice was different when he talked to Mr. Cohen.

Mr. Cohen examined the pants and then looked at me. "How did it happen?" He was calm like every day he saw wet rags for pants.

I told him that tea had spilled.

"Did you do it?"

I shook my head. "No. But what difference does it make who did it?" I was nervous, shaking like jelly, but I spoke up.

"She's lying," Sam shouted.

"I am not lying," I said.

"The girl is right. It doesn't matter who did it," Mr. Cohen said. Then he asked me a lot of questions. How long I had been in America, what I was doing, and how old I was. Then I did tell a lie. I told him I was fourteen, but I was not yet thirteen. "You look like a smart girl," he said. "I could use you around here. You could carry bundles; you can keep the place neat. There are a lot of odd jobs you can do. You want a steady job?"

"Yes, sir."

And so I got my first job in America.

Sam couldn't get over it. "You should get down on your knees and kiss the ground. Where else could a little Jewish greenhorn come with a bundle of spoiled pants and walk out with a job?"

I had to agree with him. But also I thought such a prince of a man like Mr. Cohen you find only with the Jews.

3

I worked hard for Mr. Cohen. I carried more bundles. I ran fast like I had wings. I scrubbed his office. I kept the factory neat. No job was too much for me. And little by little I was filling up Mama's bottle with coins.

I was there maybe five, six months, through the winter—when we huddled by the stove instead of looking for a breeze—and then I had an idea. One day I brought home the *shmattes* from the factory, the odds and ends of cloth from Sam's cuttings. Such a beautiful day it was. I walked through the little park, and it smelled almost like home in our village. I thought about how for Pesach Mama used to make a new dress for my sisters and me, and we'd go to *shul* in our new finery proud like peacocks. Now she had no time for anything except the knee pants.

So I decided to make something myself. But the way that material was cut up could make you crazy. Just pieces—short, long, all kinds of shapes. You could make a dress only for a freak. But finally I laid out a skirt. A gored skirt. A skirt with seams to hold the pieces together. It was beautiful. It swung when I walked like a skirt for a dancer.

Mama and Cousin Lena said it was beautiful. Even Sam had to admit it was pretty good. I asked Sam for more scraps, and I made skirts for Esther and the two little girls. Mama said we looked like little princesses.

I never wanted to take the skirt off, I liked it so

much. Mama scolded me, but one day I wore it to work. It was my lucky day. Mr. Cohen looked at my skirt. "Where'd you get that material?" he asked me.

"Just scraps. Scraps from the cuttings. Sam throws them away," I told him.

"Who made it?"

"I did. Please, I meant no harm. These pieces, they go in the garbage."

"That's what I was thinking," Mr. Cohen said. "Maybe you should make some for me, and we could try to sell them. Knee pants are not the only thing in the world. Why should we throw away good material?"

So, just like that, I was promoted to work on a machine. I didn't know it, but one, two, three, I was a designer.

I was so excited, I could hardly wait until I could go home and tell Mama my good luck. On the way I stopped and bought a box of chocolates, a beautiful box shaped like a heart with a big ribbon on top. I didn't have enough money, but Mrs. Berg, the nice lady in the store, said I could owe it to her when I told her I was celebrating.

"So, what's the holiday?" Cousin Lena asked, when I came home with the chocolates.

"Is it somebody's birthday, maybe?" Mama asked.

"No, we're celebrating my new job," I said.

And I told them what had happened. When Cousin Sam came home, he said, "So, *nu*, how much is he going to pay you?"

My heart fell. "I don't know. I didn't ask him."

Sam looked at me like I was a *shlemiel*, and I guess I was. "You'll work twice as hard for the same money. So what's to celebrate?"

"Mr. Cohen is a fine man. He'll pay me."

"Don't count on it. Fine man or not, bosses don't like to part with their money," Sam said. "One of these days we'll have a union, and they'll find out they can't get away with these sweatshops and have kids like you work for almost nothing."

"But I like to work."

"What's that got to do with it?" Sam demanded angrily. "Because you like it doesn't mean you shouldn't get paid what it's worth. You wait and see. He'll make money on those skirts, but you'll get *bubkes*."

I was a greenhorn and I was scared. All night I stayed awake thinking how I was going to ask Mr. Cohen for more money. But who was I? A foreigner, a skinny little girl who didn't speak good English, who had no education. In the morning I examined myself in the cracked mirror on the wall. What I saw was not so great. My eyes looked big and dark and sad, my cheeks were pale, another ten or fifteen pounds would have maybe given me a figure. Only my hair had any merit. It was rich and black, but there was too much of it. I needed someone to show me how to make it stylish.

All day long I waited for the right time to ask Mr. Cohen. But there was no right time. Finally, when I was ready to go home in the dark, I went up to him. Shaking in my boots, I said, "Are you going to pay me more money for making the skirts?"

"Oh, sure, sure. You'll get some more money. We've got to see how they go first. I could lose my shirt on them, too." I couldn't figure how he could lose. He had the goods and he had me, but still I thought he was a fine, honest man, so I said nothing.

Then he said, "Have you ever thought about going to school, Rachel?"

I laughed. "How could I go to school when I work all day?"

"You could go to night school. You're a smart girl You should learn good English and writing and reading. Here, you go to this place, it won't cost you nothing, and see what you can do." He wrote out a name and address, the Henry Street Settlement School, and gave it to me.

After that my whole life changed. I went to the Henry Street Settlement School, but I didn't just go to school. For me to study a little bit wasn't enough. Maybe I can never do anything halfway. Worse than Saul I was, never without a book in my hand. At the school they gave me Charles Dickens' *A Tale of Two Cities* to read. A wonderful thing like that had never happened to me. In the begining I was slow. It wasn't easy for me to understand all the words—sometimes I even went so far as to ask Saul to explain something to me—but I read that book fifty times before I realized there were hundreds more as good.

Sam laughed at me. "Why you waste your time reading? Will it help you to get a good husband, to cook chicken soup, to have babies? Better you should spend your spare time learning how to fry an egg." He would never let me forget that on Sunday, when I was making breakfast, I let the white of his egg get fried too much. Like I had committed a crime.

So the days, the weeks, and the months flew by. A year went so fast I didn't know what happened to it. I lived in a world apart from the rest of the family.

Between working and going to school I was home only for my supper at night and to go to sleep. Saturdays I spent at the library reading, reading. Always I had a book in front of me. Once in a while, with someone from the school, I went to a concert or to a coffeehouse where everybody drank tea, not coffee. Once I went to hear a socialist talk about the sweatshops and how the children were exploited. Everything he said was right, but who was going to stop it? During the year I got a little more money from Mr. Cohen (the skirts sold like hot cakes), but when I asked for more, he said that would put him out of business. What was I to do? Sam grumbled all the time, but he too had to stick to his job or his wife and children would starve.

I tried to persuade Esther to go to school, but she was too timid. She preferred to stay home with Mama and take care of the house. A real *baleboosteh* she was becoming, learning how to cook better than Mama. But Ida was something else. She and Rose went to the public school, and her handwriting was beautiful, better than mine.

One day Mama said, "Rachel, we got to have a talk."

"We talk, we talk all the time. Is there something special to talk?" I was studying for an examination, and I wished I had gone to the library instead of trying to keep my mind on my book in the crowded apartment.

"Come into the bedroom," Mama said.

Crossly, I followed her into the small room, which was no more private than any other place. "So, *nu*, what do you want to talk about?"

"We've got to move." Mama made the announcement like it was something I would object to.

"I've been saying so for a long time. But do we have the money?"

"I think we can manage." When Mama said that, I knew positively she had a boodle tucked away in her corset cover. Sometimes Mama could be foolish (like when she gave the money to the peddler), but she never spent money unless she had it. To owe anyone a nickel was to Mama a crime, and to buy on credit was only for flimsy people.

"So, find us a place to live," I said.

But Mama had more on her mind than just moving. "It's got to be a nice place, a decent home where we can invite a young man for Esther."

A bolt from out of the blue. "Esther doesn't know any young man."

"That's what I'm saying. We've got to have a proper place so I can arrange with a *shadchen* to make a good match for her."

"But Mama, Esther's only sixteen." I wasn't thinking only of Esther. I was almost fourteen, and if Mama was worrying about Esther now, I would be next. Marriage was for some dim future. Already I had become American enough to know I wanted no matchmaker to come with his fine Jewish boy who would sit and stare at me with a foolish grin on his face.

"So, you want her to be an old maid? I was seventeen when my first little Sammelle was born, may he rest in peace." Mama had two babies who died before Esther came. "We get an apartment, and right away I'll go see the *shadchen*. I've spoken to him already so he can put his mind to it."

"What about Esther? What does she think?"

Mama shrugged. "What does Esther know? She's a child. She knows nothing of the world."

"If she's a child, why are you in such a hurry?"

Mama sighed and touched her breast. "It hurts me in my heart to see such a beautiful girl with nobody. Before I die, I want to see her married, to see color in her cheeks. What kind of a life does she have with two old women like Lena and me, cleaning the house for us?"

"You're not going to die. Don't talk that way." Mama's words frightened me. I couldn't imagine life without her.

"Everyone dies. Already I'm almost forty years old. Nobody lives forever, Rachel."

A conversation like that was a worry. I didn't like to think of Mama getting old and dying, and Esther growing up and getting married. We were different, Esther and me, but we were sisters and the bond between us was strong like iron. In our veins ran the same blood, and maybe we didn't always have so much to say to each other, but we both knew that never would we want to be far apart. With Ida, it was different. She was more independent, like me, but I think she never had a family feeling like Mama's and Esther's and mine. Ida went her own way. She loved us yes, but for her a friend was as good as her family. For me it never was the same.

Afterward, I spoke with Esther and asked what did she think about moving. She knew I was really asking what did she think about Mama seeing the *shadchen*.

She looked at me with those big eyes of hers. Esther was the pretty one, with an expression like she never could say a cross word, always with her hair combed and her voice gentle. "I'll be glad," she said. "Maybe we could have our own room. Maybe Ida could sleep with Mama, and we could be by ourselves."

"Maybe you'll be getting married before another year is over," I said, not so happy about it.

Esther blushed. "I haven't met anyone yet. Maybe no one will want me. What have I got to offer?"

"You've got you." I was angry. "We've got no money, so you won't marry someone who needs your money. Mama better tell the *shadchen* right away that we don't want someone looking for a dowry. But he'll get something better than money; he'll get a prize."

Esther laughed. "You'd do better than a *shadchen*. But I'm a nobody. I can't expect much."

"Don't talk that way." It got me mad to hear Esther make a nothing of herself.

"I'm only saying the truth. I wish I was more like you. With more drive, more excitement. I'm like a mouse next to you."

"Such a mouse we should all be. You've got looks, you can cook, you know how to keep a house. You'll make some lucky man a wonderful wife. Nobody will want to marry me. I'm too bossy. But I don't care. I don't need to get married. I like to work. Someday, Esther, you'll see, I'll make a lot of money. I'll be rich enough for all of us."

Esther's face turned serious. "You will, too. I believe you will. I'll be scrubbing kitchen floors while you ride around in a fine carriage."

We both laughed at such a notion.

4

To find a place to live wasn't so easy. Mama even talked about moving out of the East Side, way uptown in the Bronx where we could have trees and grass. But for me it was too far to travel to go to work, and Ida didn't want to leave her school. I, too, didn't want to give up my studying at the Henry Street Settlement. Besides, I liked it where we were. I didn't want to live where it was quiet. I liked the noise and the excitement, the hushy-bushy of Delancey Street and Hester Street and Orchard Street. I was already feeling at home there, so why move to another place? By now I knew everyone on the street. It was nice to walk by and say hello to this one and that, to buy a hot *knish*. I liked to stop and talk to the fish man, tell him that last night's fish tasted good, to buy an apple from Mr. Schiff's pushcart, tell old Mrs. Goldberg that Mama asked how she was feeling.

At last Mama was lucky and found a place. It was brighter and sunnier than Sam's appartment, and it was on the top floor. We had to walk up six flights of stairs, but there was a toilet in the hall so we didn't have to go outside. And, best of all, Esther and I could have a room by ourselves. The kitchen was big enough so Mama could put the sewing machine in it, and there was another room for her and Ida.

Mama and Esther were packing up our things, getting ready to move soon, when I came home one night and found Ida crying her eyes out. Mama's eyes, too, were red.

"What happened?" I asked.

"Don't ask," Mama said. Then, like she was stepping on a worm, she said, "Ask your fine sister what's the matter. *Oy*, such a heartache no mother should have to suffer. I do my best to bring up respectable girls, I slave myself to the bone. Your father would cry in his grave if he knew what goes on with his baby—"

"What happened?" I yelled.

Esther answered me. "Ida's been running errands for some ladies down the street."

"So, what's the matter with that?"

Esther looked at Mama nervously. "They're not nice ladies. They bring men to their apartment."

"*Oy vay*." I was horrified. "Jewish ladies?"

"Jewish, *shiksas*, what's the difference? In the dark they're the same. But that my own daughter should get mixed up with such a gang, my baby brought up to be a good, respectable girl. . . . It's a disgrace, a shame for all of us."

Ida stopped crying long enough to speak. "They were nice to me. I didn't know what they were doing. They paid me well. So I brought them sandwiches and pickles from the delicatessen. Sometimes something from the drugstore. What's the harm in that? And they gave me a pretty name."

Mama turned on her, furious. "What's the matter? Ida isn't good enough for you? You need to get a name from a bunch of whores? *Oy vay, oy vay*." She rocked herself back and forth. "It isn't enough I have to leave my home, my village, come to a new country and leave my beloved husband's grave, and the graves of my tiny babies, but now I have to be cursed with a daughter who turns her back on her name, on her family. . . ."

"I don't like the name Ida. It's ugly. They said to change it to Inez. I like that much better. What harm does it do? It's my name. It sounds more American." Ida was drying her eyes on the kitchen towel.

"You're Jewish, not American," Esther cried.

"I'm American first," Ida said, stamping her little foot.

"*Oy, oy,* I'm going to faint. Give me my smelling salts. That I should live to hear such words from my own daughter. . . ."

I handed Mama her salts and sat down at the kitchen table. I was blaming myself. I should have paid more attention to Ida. I should have known something was going on, but I didn't want to bother. She had been bringing home candy and new ribbons for her hair. I had wondered where the money was coming from but decided that Mama was indulging her. I should have known better.

We all petted and adored Ida. Maybe feature by feature she wasn't as pretty as Esther, but she had a sparkle in her eyes and animation in her face—like a bright candle in a dark room. Her body was graceful like a ballerina's, and to watch her move was a pleasure For Ida I wanted everything I did not have. I wanted her to have a childhood with pretty clothes and pink cheeks. I wanted her to have an education, to be someone in America we would all be proud of. My hopes were pinned on Ida. Never for her to have to work in a factory and to worry about the bills. Not for her to skip from being a baby, a frightened little greenhorn, to being a woman able to take on the worries of the head of the family. In my mind, Ida was destined to marry a millionaire and be a grand lady.

Now with her red nose and red eyes, I had to laugh. "So no harm was done, Mama. We're going to move, we'll be on a different street, away from here, and Ida will forget about the fancy ladies."

"I'll never forget them," Ida mumbled. "They're nicer to me than anyone else. And my name is Inez."

"You should be ashamed of yourself." Mama was ready to explode again.

"Let's finish the packing," I said.

But I went into the bedroom and left them with the work. I had studying to do, but my mind wasn't on it. All very well for me to think that Ida should have a childhood, but I too longed to have nice dresses, to join one of the clubs for young people in the neighborhood. Often I could hear the singing and the music through the open windows and wondered what it was like not to have to go to work every day, not to feel the need to study every night.

I didn't have friends my own age. There was no time to meet any. My life was all my family, my work, and my lessons. Sometimes I wondered if we had made a mistake to come here, but in the old country there was nothing. No future, no good husband for Esther with most of the young men gone or leaving, little chance of school for Ida or me.

But my spirit was not one that stayed down for long. I kept thinking that something good was going to happen ahead, and just to walk on the streets gave me pleasure. Sometimes I went along the river and watched the boats go by and wondered where they were going. The library was my greatest pleasure. There I could stay for hours, forgetting what time it was, even what day it was. I would not live long enough to read all the books, but I was making a good start.

Once Mama got angry because I said how nice it was to see the Gentiles go to church, the whole family, men and women, on Sunday. "Only the men make a *minyan*. The women don't count in the *shul*," I mentioned to her. "On the High Holidays we women have to sit in back or upstairs if there's an upstairs."

"What's the matter, you don't like your religion no more? In America you like the church better?" Mama was burning.

"Nothing to do with America," I said. "Is it a crime to make a remark? To have an opinion?"

"Such remarks I don't have to listen to."

The truth was, things were different in America. In the old country the rabbi married you, divorced you, kept all the records. He knew when everyone was born, and he settled all the arguments. In America everything was arranged by the law. The rabbi was nothing with the government.

But that had little to do with some of the funny ideas I was getting in my head.

Before the High Holidays we moved. It wasn't hard to get settled in our new apartment since our belongings were very few. Except for the dishes. Our house was kosher like always: the meat dishes separate from the milk dishes, every pot and pan separate. So dishes we had plenty: *flayshedig* and *milchedig* and also two sets for Pesach. What Mama wanted most was an ice-

box to keep our food in, and we found a secondhand
one we bought.

It was possible to get the big squares of ice up to
the sixth floor in the dumbwaiter. But the dumbwaiter
terrified Mama for fear that Ida, who loved to work
the ropes, would lean over too far and fall down from
our floor to the basement. She put a bolt across the
door, which didn't make sense since Ida could open it
as easily as anyone.

Yom Kippur was a holiday I liked. I felt clean in
my spirit and body, like starting off with a new slate.
Fasting I didn't mind—only Ida complained all day
she was hungry. It was good for my health, and I liked
that everybody, not just me, had sins to atone for, even
the rabbi and his wife.

We broke our fast at Cousin Lena's. At the table
she asked Mama when the *shadchen* was coming with
the young man to introduce to Esther. Esther turned
pale.

"Soon. Very soon," Mama told her.

Ida giggled. "Esther's scared."

"I'm not," Esther said, indignant. "Why should I
be?"

"Maybe he'll be ugly," Ida said.

"Don't talk that way." Mama glanced at Esther.
"The *shadchen's* a fine man. Only an educated man,
I told him. Someone from a good family."

"What will he want with me?" Esther asked.

"What's your hurry?" Cousin Sam demanded. "In
America girls don't get married so young. And they
pick their own husbands. You're old-fashioned," he
told Mama.

Mama glared at him. "I do things my way, you do

them yours. And," she added, turning to Esther, "we don't have to take the first one who comes along. If you don't like that one, he'll find another."

"How will she know? Just meeting him isn't enough," I said.

"She'll know," Mama said. "She doesn't have to decide right away the minute she meets him. She'll have plenty of time. They'll spend time together."

Esther did look scared. She looked at me like I was her only hope in life. "I don't want to be alone with him. You stay with me, Rachel. I won't know what to say to him."

Mama laughed. "A man doesn't like a woman who talks too much. You don't have to make speeches. If you're religious and pretty, that's enough."

"Not me," Ida said. "When it's my turn to meet a man, I'm going to tell him what I think. And no *shadchen*'s going to pick him out for me either."

"Listen to her talk," Mama said. "A grown-up lady already with ideas."

"She's not the only one," I said to Mama. "Me, too. I don't think a woman has to keep her mouth shut."

"*Oy, oy.* Two wise guys I've got. You want to marry a *shlemiel* who's going to listen to a woman prattle all day?"

"I don't prattle. I'm as smart as any man. Smarter," I added, looking directly at Saul.

He looked up and gave me his stupid grin. "You wish it," he said.

"Maybe too smart you're getting to be," Mama said.

Something happened soon after the Holidays to make me wonder what was going on with me. One day I was walking by myself several blocks from our house, and I smelled something cooking that made the juices run in my mouth. I had never smelled anything so good before. It came from a cart where a man was selling strips of roast meat. I bought a few slices on a role. *Oy*, such a taste, like eating something from heaven. I gobbled it up. Then I asked the man what was the meat. "Pork, roast pork. What else?" he told me.

I almost fainted. My stomach turned over and I gagged. So help me God, I expected to be struck down right there on the street. I stood frozen like someone already dead.

The man grinned at me, his eyes gleaming like a devil. "Taste good, eh?"

I went to the curb and spat, but I could not get the taste from my mouth.

For days I was in despair. Deep in my heart I think I knew before I ate that it was forbidden. Otherwise, why would I have waited until I finished before I asked? I felt a curse had been put upon me, a lump of evil was growing inside my body. Every day I waited to be struck down, but nothing happened. So I began to wonder was it really a sin to eat milk with meat, to eat a piece of meat that wasn't kosher? In America there were other immigrants living side by side with us: Italians, Irish, Chinese. They ate everything and they didn't die. Why us? *Oy*, such disturbing thoughts for my young mind. I didn't know what to do with them, so I pushed them aside.

But that wasn't all. My head was beginning to get filled with so many questions that sometimes I thought better I should not think at all. Mr. Cohen had moved to a bigger loft and had a real factory going. Fourteen hours a day I worked at my machine making skirts, with the baster behind me and the finisher in between. Twenty-five skirts a day he wanted us to make, and always we were driving to keep up with the other three teams he had working the same. It was impossible. By the time we finished twenty, sometimes twenty-one, twenty-two garments, we were so tired we could hardly breathe. But it was always more, more. For a dozen we got seventy cents. The room was dark, crowded, filled with the smoke from the men's cigarettes, the smell of the beer they drank—it was unhealthy.

Sometimes I read the socialist-labor-party newspaper, and sometimes I went to one of the meetings always being held on the East Side. There was much talk in them of unions, of exploitation, of the bosses making profits off the backs and sweat of the workers. I could see it was true. What I could not see was how they were going to turn it around. Never could the workers make the same profit as the bosses, no matter how hard they worked. I agreed with everything they said, but for myself, I wanted to be a boss. I could see how Mr. Cohen was getting richer and richer by the way we worked, and I thought there was nothing so special about him. I was the one who had shown him how to make the skirts in the first place. Why shouldn't I be the one making the money?

When I said so, Mama said I talked like a man. "Why a man?" I asked her. "A woman doesn't have any brains?"

"A woman should be in the home. Should take care of her husband and children," Mama said.

"Where is it written in the book that way? A woman is born with a head like a man, only below is she different," I said. "She is made smarter than a man. She has the same head *and* a place to carry a baby. She is more than a man."

Mama laughed at me and said I was *meshugge*. *Meshugge* or not, I thought, I work on the machine as good as anyone, and someday I'll show her. I'll show her my brain is as good as Mr. Cohen's. Better.

5

Mama didn't waste much time. We weren't in our new apartment more than a few weeks when she announced that the *shadchen* was coming the following Sunday afternoon to meet Esther. Esther turned pale. "What does he have to meet me for? He's not going to marry me."

"You think he should sell someone he never laid eyes on? He's not that kind of a man. You want he should bring over a boy he never knew?"

"I don't want to be sold. I don't want to meet him."

"Who said someone is selling you? Such an idea. Just an expression, you should pay no attention. He wants to know what you like, what your preferences are. You'll see. You'll like him."

It was not in Esther to argue, but all week she crept around like on Sunday she was going to the death chair. I tried to cheer her up. "No one says you have to marry someone he brings over," I told her. "Don't let Mama or anyone talk you into anything. If you don't like a boy, just say so. You're the one who has to decide."

We were in our room together with the door closed. That room was a *mitzva*, a gift we cherished. There Esther and I told each other our deepest secrets, we confided our dreams and our worries. What each of us wanted was different, like night from day. Much as Esther trembled at the thought of meeting a future husband, she admitted that getting married and having her own home was what she dreamed of all the time. "But what if I pick the wrong one?" she said to me that night when we were talking, sitting on our bed with the big comforter tucked around us.

"You'll have to not be in a hurry. You'll have to take your time. I wish there was some test we could think of so you could tell."

"Maybe there is." Esther blushed. "Don't laugh at me, Rachel, but I think that if a boy kissed me, I'd know whether I liked him or not. Sometimes I look at boys, at men too, and I think that if he kissed me it would make me sick, but with others I think it might be very nice."

I looked at her with big eyes. "Such thoughts really go on in your head?"

Esther nodded. "You think I'm wicked?"

"No." I wasn't thinking of Esther; I was thinking of myself. "Do you suppose there's something wrong with me? Such things never enter my mind. I think, How can we get more skirts out of the material? How can I finish more skirts? How can I make more money?"

"That's because you're smart and I'm not. I wonder how will I fix up my own kitchen, what things I'll cook for my husband, what will it be like to have a child. But you have to have a life beside just work, Rachie. That's not enough."

"I have my books. When I read I forget everything else. But marriage—I don't know. Maybe sometime if I fall in love. . . ."

"You wouldn't have a *shadchen*, would you?"

I didn't know how to answer I didn't want to hurt Esther. I knew that I wouldn't, but for Esther I honestly thought it was the best. She was too timid, too shy to meet anyone on her own. And, after all, getting married was what she wanted most. "Maybe not," I said, "but. . . ."

Esther laughed. "But for me it's right because I'm a dummy."

"You're not a dummy. But I think maybe you need someone to give you a push."

By Sunday we were all nervous. "Why is everyone so excited?" Mama said, sweeping the kitchen floor for the hundredth time. "So what? So a neighbor is dropping in to see us for a little visit. You girls never saw a man before?"

"Is that why you took out your best teapot?" Ida teased. "Just for any old neighbor?"

"Rachel, taste one of the *shnecken* and see if they're all right," Esther asked me. She had been baking Friday and again this morning for the event.

"No," Mama shrieked "The *shnecken* are fine, don't worry. She'll spoil the way the dish looks."

"I don't know why you're all so excited," I said, as nervous as the rest of them. "Today only the *shadchen* is coming. What are you going to do when he brings the young man?"

"I'll faint," Esther said.

Mr. Shapiro, the *shadchen*, was a sporty-looking man. He had a beautiful, curly reddish mustache, lots of blond hair, and carried a fine cane. Also he was full of jokes and talked all the time. "So, you want to get married," he said to Esther. "Your mother's not treating you good, eh? But I bet she made all these cakes. *Oy*, are they delicious! They melt in your mouth. I should find you a husband, Mrs. Ginsberg, not your daughter. A fine woman like you who bakes so good. . . ." He was stuffing his mouth so he had to stop talking.

"Esther baked the *shnecken*," Mama said. "She's a fine cook. Me, I don't want a husband anymore. I'm too old for that kind of thing. Only I want to see my daughters taken care of."

"I'll take care of them, don't worry. Each one in due time. Stand up, Esther, let me see what you look like. All crumbled up in the chair like that, what can I tell? Once I took a fine young man to meet a girl, a real beauty, a face like a rose. But the boy objected because she had a small limp, nothing at all. So I told him it's only when she walks. . . ." He laughed heartily at his joke while poor Esther stood up for a couple of seconds and sat down again.

He talked to Esther a little more, but what he learned about her I could not say. She hardly spoke, and I was afraid he was going to get discouraged. But not Mr. Shapiro. After a little while he said, "Excuse me, girls, but your mother and I have a little business to discuss. Marriage is not only love. But believe me, my couples are happy. Every one of them, like a marriage made in heaven. I don't do this for the money. I like to help young people, old people too, find the right mate. But marriage is also a serious business, and when the bills come in, love can fly out. So a little business we have to take care of."

Mama waved us away, and the three of us went into Esther's and my bedroom. No sooner was the door closed than Esther burst into tears. *"Oy, oy,"* she sobbed, "I don't like him and he didn't like me. I don't want to marry anyone he picks out."

"Don't," Ida said. "I wouldn't. He's never going to find me a husband."

"He won't have to for years, Ida," I told her. "You're still a baby, only nine years old."

"How many times have I told you? My name is Inez, not Ida. I'm not going to answer to Ida anymore."

"All right, all right." I was worried about Esther and I wasn't going to argue with Ida, Inez. I didn't care what she wanted to be called. "What makes you think he didn't like you?" I asked Esther. "He ate enough of your cake to kill a horse."

"I could tell." She had stopped sobbing so hard and was wiping her face. "Rachel, what should I do?"

"Wait. Wait and see who he brings over. Maybe he'll bring someone you'll like. You're not marrying the *shadchen.*"

"Oh, God, I wish we had never come to America."

"At home there are *shadchens* too. It would be the same."

"Maybe at home it would be someone I knew. I wouldn't have to meet a stranger."

"This is more exciting." I wanted to cheer her, but I knew I wouldn't want to be in her shoes.

The minute the *shadchen* left we all flew out to Mama. "What did he say?" Esther asked.

Mama was all smiles. "He said for such a beautiful, refined girl he wouldn't bring just anybody. He said he had to think carefully who would be good enough to make a match."

"He really said that?" Esther was blushing.

"Is he going to say she's no good? He says that to everyone," Ida piped up. I was thinking the same thing, but I wanted to kick her for saying it.

Mama glared at her. "Look at your sister. You see for yourself what he says is so. What he tells other people I don't care. For my Esther he speaks the truth."

"I wish it was all over," Esther said. "I wish I was married already."

"Now you're in a hurry," Mama said. "Before you didn't want the *shadchen* should come. But it isn't going to be so fast. Even after you meet a right young man, the wedding isn't going to be one, two, three. Everything has to be arranged, prepared."

For a few weeks everything was quiet in the house. But at night in our room Esther worried out loud. "See, I told you, no one wants a poor girl like me. A *schlemiel* who doesn't open her mouth, who sits in a chair like a dummy."

"He said he was going to take his time to find the right man."

"So where is he looking? In Boston? Right here it's so big, he can't find someone?"

"One minute you say you don't want to meet someone, and the next you worry he doesn't bring someone right away. You should not be so up and down like a seesaw."

But Mr. Shapiro didn't forget about our Esther. Before the month was out Mama said that on Saturday evening Mr. Shapiro was coming over to introduce someone. *Oy vay.* Such excitement you can't imagine. Again the house got scrubbed like it was for a wedding, again Esther fidgeted all week before and baked like for an army on Friday. Mama and I stayed up two nights sewing a new dress for her, a beautiful blue silk trimmed with velvet bands. Saturday morning she bathed and washed her hair, and I brushed it until it shone. No one ate much supper Saturday night. Even Ida—called Inez—only picked at her food, although she kept saying, "Why is everyone so nervous? Maybe a boy she won't even like is coming."

At eight o'clock sharp we could hear them climbing up the stairs. Esther ran into our room, and Mama looked like she was going to faint. "Go get Esther," she whispered to me. "Such a *meshuggeneh* family I never knew. . . ."

I made for our room when the knock came on the door. "Esther, you've got to come out," I pleaded with her.

"You go first. Tell me what he looks like."

"You want I should take a picture? Come on. I can't look at him and then come back here."

Esther was pushing me toward the door. "You go first. Go and say you'll call me."

She pushed me out the door. "Ah, Miss Ginsberg. Esther, I want you to meet. . . ." Mr. Shapiro was looking right at me.

"I'm not Esther," I said quickly. "She'll be here in a few minutes."

Mr. Shapiro was annoyed. "Ah, this is another Miss Ginsberg. This is Mr. Isidor Solomon."

"How do you do?" We shook hands. His hands were damp and it wasn't hot. So he too was nervous. In all our talk we never thought that maybe the boy would be fidgeting all week, that he would be dreading a visit to meet a possible bride. Already I felt better. What was there to be afraid of? A boy sweating with nervousness. . . . I stole another look at him. Not a boy, a man. Maybe twenty-three, twenty-four years old. Not so bad looking either. Not short, not tall, maybe a little plump, but with bright brown eyes and a mop of curly hair. A nice, friendly face, now a little pale perhaps.

I ran back to Esther. "He's all right. He's nice. No pimples on his face, nothing funny. Come on out. Don't be nervous. He's more scared than you are."

I took her by the hand and dragged her to the door and gave her a push. She almost fell into the room.

Mr. Shapiro introduced them, and they shook hands. Esther sat down with her hands in her lap, sitting up straight like a stick. "Mr. Solomon comes from Grodno," Mr. Shapiro said.

"Ah, not so far from our village. Our town," Mama corrected herself, not wanting them to think we were peasants.

She and Mr. Shapiro did most of the talking. The two main people sat trying to look at each other without seeming to. Like two people on the stage they were acting, like every day they sat dressed up pretending not to see each other. Now I was nervous thinking they would stay this way forever. We would all get to be old people sitting in this room listening to Mama put on airs and watching Mr. Shapiro nod his head but not believe a word she said.

"We had a beautiful home," Mama said, "and it was sad for me to give it up. But I wanted my daughters to live in a country where they could be educated and meet fine young people. For me, I would have been happy to stay home, but for them I wanted the best, I wanted every opportunity."

I thought of our simple cottage and how anxious Mama was to leave it, and I wanted to laugh.

Finally she jumped up. "*Oy*, such a terrible hostess. We must have some tea, some fruit, some beautiful cakes Esther baked. Such a cook. It's a wonder we're all not rolling in fat from the way she cooks and bakes. You like to eat, Mr. Solomon?"

"Yes, I do. Very much. I miss my mother's cooking."

"You have no mother?" Mama was ready to cry for his dead mother she never knew.

"Oh, yes. But she is home, in Grodno. Only I came over."

"*Oy*, you poor boy. You must come have dinner with us. You eat in restaurants?"

"Most of the time," he said.

"That must be very expensive," Mama said, giving Esther a look that spoke books. "And no parents, no family here. A wife would have no *machetunim*," Mama murmured as if to herself, but loud enough for Esther's ears.

"No mother-in-law," Mr. Shapiro echoed cheerfully.

Esther made out that she didn't hear. "It must be very lonely for you," she said timidly.

Mr. Solomon really looked at her then. "It *is* very lonely," he said.

Their eyes met, and I felt like suddenly something beautiful was happening between them. They weren't afraid anymore. Esther's face broke into a smile, and he smiled back, and I knew that we were going to have a wedding.

After that it didn't matter who talked, that Mr. Solomon spilled a little tea on his vest, that Esther's cakes disappeared like pennies in front of a beggar. The two principal characters grinned at each other foolishly, and Mama and Mr. Shapiro were *plotzing* like they had invented love. Before Mr. Solomon left it was arranged he should come for dinner the following Friday night.

So Esther's courtship began. Soon Iz became a regular boarder; not only Friday night but almost every other night too he had his meals with us. I didn't mind; he was a nice enough young man, and sometimes he brought a bag of candy for Inez. (By this time we were sick of arguing and everyone except Mama forgot she was Ida and called her Inez.) But I said to Mama, "What are they waiting for? They might as well get married."

"Not such a hurry," Mama said. "First I have to save money for the wedding, and they should take their time."

Inez was more worried about the money than I was. "If Mama spends everything on Esther, there won't be anything left for you and me," she said. "It's not fair."

"Me, I don't care. I don't want a wedding anyhow, *if* I ever get married. By your time, there'll be more money."

What I didn't like so much was the way Mama fussed over Iz like he was royalty. "Save the *pupik* of the chicken for Iz, give him the liver, don't cook the cabbage too long, Iz doesn't like it. . . ." Everything in our house all of a sudden was for Iz. That irked me. "I suppose when they get married, I'll have to move out of my room," I grumbled. There was no question but that the couple would live with us. "You should have found someone who could afford his own place to live," I said to Mama.

"Beggars aren't choosers. Be glad she's got such a fine young man. A millionaire my daughters can't have." Esther seemed content enough to look forward to marriage with Iz and to have him move into our old room with her. But such a future didn't appeal to me.

Iz worked in a small factory that made children's dresses. He said it was better than making a finished garment at home, although on the machine the work was more monotonous. He talked big about the union coming in, like it would solve all the problems. Maybe someday it would, but in the meantime he was lucky to bring home five, six dollars a week. From that he had to pay his rent and pay Mama two dollars a week for his food. That was when he was working. Half the year he could be laid off, because people bought children's dresses for special occasions like holidays and graduations and confirmations.

Already Esther lived in constant fear that one day Iz would join a group of strikers and get his head bashed in by the police. Like when strikers wrecked the bakeshop of Philip Federman on Orchard Street and the police smashed heads right and left with their nightsticks. The same could happen with the garment workers where conditions were maybe worse.

I thought, Did I come to America to live in a dark, crowded little tenement and smell cabbage and onions cooking all day? To hear the machines going behind the doors and to work from seven in the morning until ten at night while ladies uptown on Fifth Avenue rode in fine carriages and wore fancy gowns? I wanted part of it. I wasn't content to marry another Iz, to watch my babies grow up with the same hardships that we were suffering. I was young and strong, and I had dreams that soared above the narrow streets and the life of a Jewish girl. I was not willing to accept passively whatever life offered. I wasn't afraid of work, but from it I wanted comfort and ease and the peace of mind that money could bring. Around me I could see that most of the problems of human life—sickness, arguments, bitterness, discontent—all had poverty as their source. Money alone did not cure everything—one had to have his religion and a conscience—but not to worry each week if there was food to eat and money for the rent went a long way to make life less of a burden.

I could not share my thoughts with Esther. Now, with Iz in our lives, a wall was growing between us. Her happiness shone in her face, and yet I kept seeing the darker side, the years of hardship and struggle ahead, and I wished I could warn her. But I had nothing to suggest. As Mama said, millionaires didn't grow on Delancey Street.

There was only one other choice: to make the money myself. America was the land of opportunity, they said, so why not for me? Changes were taking place. Fewer sweatshops and more factories where the hours were not so long yet more work could be turned out, and so a little more money for the workers. The union was organizing some of the factories, and their improvements would help us all. Still, only the bosses could get rich. And who were they? Jewish men who, like myself, had come to this country poor, with maybe no education. But they worked hard, bought up a few machines, and set themselves up in business. When they got money they bought the tenements and made more money. Maybe they too had dreams like mine, to give their children better than what they had, and if others could do it, why not me? A woman didn't have to stick to the sewing machine or sew on the buttons. At the Henry Street Settlement I could see the women often learned faster than the men, so why not in business too?

6

So the winter went by. Our pleasure at the end of the work week was Shabbes when Mama lit the candle and said a prayer over the *challa*. Even our unappetizing room looked pretty with the light from the candles. Also, we now had mantles for the gas jets that gave a nice glow to the room, better than when there was nothing around the gas fixture. By this time, Iz went to our *shul*, nothing more than a meeting in a store, and without him many times there would have been no *minyan*. So many little congregations like ours on the East Side. Often I thought if we could all get together and build a fine temple it would be better. But everyone was poor, and I guess God heard our prayers the same as from a fancy synagogue.

Little by little I dragged out of Mama why she was putting off the wedding. Mama and her secrets. A little bag of money she'd said nothing about. All this time she had it in her mind to set Iz up in a business of his own once the marriage took place.

"The *shadchen* is right," Mama said. "How else could a young couple get ahead? He persuaded me. I saved it so my Esther could have a good start with an honest man."

"And what about your Inez and your Rachel?"

"An Inez I don't have. For my Ida there's plenty of time." Mama's face dimpled in a smile. "For my Rachel I won't need any money. Someone will pay me to get her. Such a girl a man doesn't find every day."

I laughed with her. She used to say no man would have me. "I don't see them knocking on our door."

"You don't look, that's your trouble. My Esther's a good girl, but you've got something extra. You've got a fire burning in you that is going to give a man trouble in his heart. But trouble that he will like. Looks you got plenty, a figure you're getting, but with the brains you should learn to go a little easy. I've lived longer than you. A man doesn't like for his wife to be smarter than he is, and if she is, what he doesn't know won't hurt him. So to be smart, sometimes you should play dumb. You understand?"

I laughed. "Maybe I'm smart enough to do without a man."

"Don't say such a thing. A woman without a man is like—like I don't know what. Like a house with nothing in it. Empty. No good."

"Still, you haven't told me why you're waiting for the wedding. You have your bag of money."

"It's not enough," Mama said. "I promised more."

I shook my head with despair. "They want to squeeze the blood out of you. Does Esther know?"

Mama paled. "God forbid. Esther must not know. Esther is in love, God bless her. Iz is, too. I think now he would not care about the money. With Mr. Shapiro it's business. And a bargain's a bargain. I gave my word."

Such a person Mama was. I thought if I had a fire in me I got it from her. Except with her, it was different. A slow, burning flame that kept us all warm—working hard, never complaining, lonesome for the old country yet curious about the new. Iz brought the Jewish paper to our house now, and I noticed Mama reading it from beginning to end. Sometimes she laughed out loud; sometimes she cried from the stories she read.

My fire wasn't slow. Sometimes I felt consumed with all the desires burning inside me—dreams for Mama to have peace and comfort for her old age, a fine house for Esther and Iz, an education for Inez. And for myself so many things, but mainly to make something of my life, to make a mark so people would look at me and say, "There goes Rachel Ginsberg." I wanted to be a person of importance, and in America for people to make way for you on the street you needed wealth.

In the spring Iz came to Mama and said he wanted to get married. He didn't want to wait any longer, money or no money. If he moved in with us, which already had been decided, he didn't have to have his business right away. When the money was there, would be time enough.

Mama wasn't hard to persuade because she worried that if they waited too long something no good would happen. "I can see with my own eyes," she said. "What's natural is natural, so it's better they get married."

So a June wedding was planned. *Oy vay iz mir*, such planning. Every night when I came home from work there was some new idea, some new argument.

Should the wedding be in our *shul* that wasn't really a *shul*? Should Mama hire a hall that was bigger?

"Who is there to invite?" I asked. "So many relatives we don't have here."

Mama was marking down names: Cousin Sam and Lena, Sam's brother from Newark, Lena's niece and nephew, the rabbi and his wife, people from our congregation, friends Mama made in the neighborhood, friends Iz had from his factory and from the club he went to. Also it turned out Iz had an uncle and aunt in Philadelphia, and they had children and more relatives. "Maybe you should put a notice in the paper for all of New York to come," Inez said. Always she was worried that Mama was spending too much money on Esther.

"I want she should have a fine wedding," Mama said. "If Papa was alive, may he rest in peace, he'd want the same."

Iz wanted the best hall. What did he care? It wasn't his money being spent.

Only Esther didn't argue. She knew, as I did, that in the end Mama would do what she wanted. "Whatever they decide is all right with me," Esther said.

Only on one thing, Esther would not budge. She refused absolutely to have her head shaved and to wear a *shaytl*.

"I'll do whatever you want. I'll go to the *mikva* gladly. When I have my own home, it will be kosher. I'll always keep Shabbes; every Friday night I'll light the candles. But I will not have my head shaved." Gentle Esther was firm like a rock.

Mama pleaded with her. She got angry and screamed. "Better you should take a knife and cut out my heart. What have I done to deserve a daughter who throws away her religion like an old shoe? I tear my heart out to give her a beautiful Jewish wedding, and all of a sudden she wants to live like a *goy*."

"I'm not living like a *goy*." Esther spoke quietly. "Iz doesn't want me to shave my head. He is my husband or will be, and it's my duty to obey him."

That got Mama even madder. She knew Esther was trying to outfox her with pious words. "*Oy, oy,* so already she has to obey her husband. He's not your husband yet," Mama yelled, "and what does he know? Another wise guy who thinks because he shaved off his beard he's American. You think he'll love you better with your own hair? Believe me, in the dark he won't know. You'll be thankful if he doesn't love you so much that every year you have a baby."

Esther was shocked by Mama's outburst, but she wouldn't budge. She was worried that in her sleep Mama would come and cut off her hair, so every night we put a chair in front of our door to make sure we'd wake up if Mama tried to do such a thing.

Finally the day of the wedding drew near. The weather had been so hot you could die. We were all praying for rain to cool it off. Mama said she hoped not on the wedding day, because then everyone would think Esther was a *nosher*. One of Mama's *bobbe-mysehs*.

The day before the wedding still no rain. The *chuppa* was ready. Three cousins of Iz and a friend from where he worked were going to hold it for the couple. The cooking and baking were still going on in our house and in Cousin Lena's. Mama had ordered a wedding cake from the bakery, but at home she had made dozens of *knishes*, roast chickens, cookies, God knows what all she and Lena prepared. The wedding gown and our dresses—Ida's, Mama's, and mine—were hanging in the bedroom and every time Mama looked at them she wept that she hadn't brought her own wedding veil from home. "How could I have forgotten such a thing," she

wailed, and she would *hok* us *a tchynik* for an hour
again about it.

Early on the morning of her wedding day, I went
with Esther to the *mikva*. It was still cool and fresh on
the street before the heat came up out of the earth and
the pavement. As we walked down the street everyone
smiled and waved and gave us a blessing.

We didn't talk yet I could see that Esther was nervous.
Me, too. All of a sudden I was worried that Mama had
pushed Esther too much, that maybe Iz wasn't the right
person. I was nervous too about us all living together
in one house. A man in the house was going to make
everything different. Because I made the most money, I
had been what you might call "the boss," the head of
the house, even though I wasn't the oldest. Mama was
still really the boss, but more and more she liked me to
make decisions. Iz was all right, a good man who didn't
drink or swear, but he wasn't the smartest man in the
world. I could see already that about many things we
wouldn't agree. Mama would stand up for Iz, and cer-
tainly Esther would, so I would be outvoted. It should
be a beautiful wedding, I thought, but afterward it may
not be so good.

In the *mikva* I let Esther alone. She said her prayers,
she bathed and I bathed, but from the look on her face
she could have been going to a funeral instead of her
wedding.

Back home when we were getting dressed, Esther suddenly sat down on the bed in her petticoat and looked
as if she was going to cry. "I'm scared, Rachel," she said.

"You've got nothing to be afraid of," I said, knowing
full well in her shoes I would be scared too.

She looked around the room. "Tonight, right here

in this room, I'll be getting undressed with Iz. How can I do that?"

"It'll be dark. He won't see you."

"Has a boy ever kissed you?" she asked.

I looked at her like she was crazy. "Where would a boy have kissed me? You think in the factory we make love?" I laughed. "You should see the men in that place. You wouldn't wish them on your sister."

"I didn't know. You know so much more than I do. You would know what to do better than me. I'll be ashamed in front of Iz, ashamed I'll act stupid."

"Maybe he won't know any more than you."

Esther giggled. "That wouldn't be such a blessing. One of us should know what to do."

"Enough people have already gotten married, so maybe it comes to you. It's an instinct. Otherwise there wouldn't be so many babies in the world. Maybe right away you won't know, but it will come, I think." I turned my face away because I felt shy. Then I said what was on my mind. "Esther, when it comes my turn, if I ever get married, will you tell me? You'll know by then. Would you?"

"If I know, I'll tell you."

"Promise?"

"I promise."

We hooked up each other's dresses and were admiring ourselves, when all of a sudden she took me in her arms and hugged me hard. "Rachel, don't let anything change between us. Promise you won't."

"I'll try," I said. I hugged her hard. But I knew in my heart that once she was a married woman, things would change. Things could not remain the same.

* * *

Such a beautiful wedding, like out of a book. Mama cried and so did I. Inez giggled when Iz stepped on the ritual glass so hard it shattered into a million pieces. Still sixteen, Esther looked so young that I couldn't believe she was getting married already, and Mama cried because Papa wasn't there to see her. Cousin Sam gave her away and acted like a big *macher*. Mama had decided on a hall so that music could be played, and everyone drank wine and ate and danced, especially Inez. Like a butterfly, she flitted all over and danced with young and old. They stayed until after midnight, and Esther looked like she might faint from exhaustion.

I didn't want to go home. I kept thinking of Esther and Iz going into our old bedroom and closing the door, and my heart trembled. A wall would go up between Esther and me, and I was filled with sorrow.

For Esther, too, I was worried. Would Iz be good to her or would he laugh at her ignorance? Would he be gentle with her? I had more knowledge of the world than she did. I listened to the men in the factory, heard them swear and laugh at their coarse jokes, watched them drink their beer and make eyes at the girls. When I went home I tried to walk with one of the girls for fear a man would follow me in the dark. The city could be a fearful place for young girls, and I knew that a man, even an educated man, which Iz was not, could be rough with a girl. Especially someone so pure like our Esther.

The bridal couple left before the rest of us, and when Mama, Inez, and I got home the door was already closed. Mama had the same thoughts that I did. After she sent Inez into their room to go to bed, she sat with me and her face was sad. She rocked back and forth, murmuring, "*Oy vay, oy vay,* my little girl."

"They'll be all right," I told her. "Don't worry, Mama."

She looked at me like she was angry, like maybe I said something wrong. "All right? What do you know about all right? All right's not enough."

She was telling me something. Years of all right she'd had, and for Esther she wanted more. We sat there until her head was nodding, and I helped her get up and into her bed. For a long time I sat by myself thinking how funny life was. On Esther's wedding day I should be happy, but instead I was feeling sad like I did when Papa died. So foolish, but when you feel, you forget smart, foolish. It doesn't matter. You just feel.

7

Soon it was like Iz had always been living with us. No different. Maybe a little more crowded but also a little more money.

More and more Iz was talking about the union. Every night he went to meetings and came home to give us speeches. Excited like a kid he was, a real socialist, full of ideas of how the workers would take over and make the money instead of the bosses. With the workers it would be divided evenly, he said, or by what each one did, instead of one boss making all the profit. A good idea. But I didn't know how they were going to do it. I could see there were a lot of little bosses who weren't making much more money than the people on the machines. Maybe someday, when there were big factories with a lot of workers, the union would have a say.

But I admired Iz, although I was what you call skeptical. Esther was plain worried. Maybe two years after they were married, when she was already big with her baby, Iz didn't come home from work one night. We waited and waited. Esther was white like a sheet, and I said I would go look for him. It was already dark, and wrapped in my shawl I walked to where he worked. Long blocks. When I got there the place was closed. People on the street told me the men had gone out on strike and the police had come and some of the men got hurt. Like the Cossacks in the old country, the police had beat them up. Those who were hurt had been taken to the hospital.

In the dark, I walked to the hospital. Such a walk I never want to have again in my life, a young girl alone in the street. Not so bad where it was familiar, but I had to go on blocks I'd never seen before. Besides worrying about Iz, I was scared. Someone maybe would hit me over the head, and Mama and Esther would never find Iz or me. I was afraid to run, afraid to walk too slow, and all the time I kept looking behind to make sure no stranger was following. I thought I'd be walking all night before I came to the hospital.

There, I tried to explain who I was looking for. But no one understood my broken English, and everyone told me I should wait. Wait. Who wanted to wait when a sister was home maybe having her baby before her time, a brother-in-law maybe dying? So I waited.

When I could wait no longer, I went up to a young man with a beard—he looked like a nice Jewish man—dressed in white, and again I told him my story. He said he'd see what he could do. And he did. He took me into a room, and there was Iz. I wanted to faint when I saw him, his head bandaged, looking like he was already half dead.

"Take me home," Iz said to me.

He could hardly stand up and he said take me home, just like that. The doctor said no, that he had to stay overnight. Iz argued with the doctor. I didn't open my mouth. I didn't know which one was right so I kept still. Iz was stubborn and said he was all right. We didn't have to walk all the way home; part of the way we could take a trolley car. The doctor had other things to do, and he said, "I won't be responsible," and walked away.

The doctor won't be responsible. But all of a sudden a frightened young girl, who knows from nothing, is taking a man with a broken head through the streets of New York at midnight. Maybe it wasn't midnight. Maybe it was only nine, ten o'clock, but that was neither here nor there. The time was not the problem. What if he should die on my hands? *Oy*, even a stubborn man should listen to a doctor.

We took a trolley and we walked and, thank God, at last we got to our house. But then, I thought, the six flights of stairs is too much. The way Iz is dragging his feet he will never make it. So I got the smart idea to put him on the dumbwaiter. Iz looked at me like I was crazy, but he was already half dead and so he agreed. I helped him get on, all twisted up like a pretzel, and I ran upstairs to pull him up.

And that was how, the very night his son, Nathan, was born, Iz arrived home. Like a Turk swathed in bandages, he was, crawling out of the dumbwaiter.

Inez had already run for the midwife, Mama was boiling water, and Esther was in bed, screaming her head off.

I went to sit with Esther, but Iz we would not allow into the room. She would take one look at him, and God knows what would come out of her womb. *Oy*, such a night.

Inez came back with a dark-skinned midwife, a mulatto maybe, and Iz, the big socialist, yelled he didn't want a black to deliver his baby. Who cared? Black, white, pink, or blue. Her name was Mary, and God bless her forever. She knew what she was doing, and in three hours Esther gave birth to a beautiful baby boy. Mama took the baby out for Iz to see, and he acted like he had done all the work. He went so crazy he even hugged the midwife like she was his sister.

After that night there was plenty of trouble. But we Jews are used to trouble. There are some who say that if we didn't have trouble to make us strong, we'd have been gone two thousand years ago. Maybe so. For myself, I could do with a little less.

The apartment didn't grow. The walls stayed the same. But the four of us who had started to live in it had now become six, and there were the bottles for the baby, because frail Esther had no milk. Iz wanted the baby to be named Chaim after his brother, but this time Esther stood by Mama and the baby was named Nathan after Papa.

Besides the aggravation of being so crowded, one on top of another, money was the big *tsorah*. Where was it going to come from? For the *bris* Mama and Iz insisted on another party. (Esther said she didn't care; she was so engrossed with her baby, nothing else mattered.) For the *mohel* money was needed too. Somehow Mama managed, and we had a *bris* like money was found on the street. From the beginning, little Nathan was treated like a prince.

But Iz had no job, and soon I too was laid off. That's the way it was in the cloak-and-suit business. Twice a year it was like a race for everyone to get out the spring line and the fall line, and then business would slacken and the workers got laid off. Where I worked, downtown in the little sweatshops, it was worse than uptown around twenty-fifth, twenty-sixth, and twenty-seventh streets. There the factories were bigger, and the union, the ILGWU, was beginning to organize. Cousin Sam was doing all right. The cutters were king. No one wanted to lose a good cutter who could cut six or seven garments at a time. But I couldn't get a job as one because the cutting knives they used instead of scissors now were too heavy for a woman.

Such a year I wouldn't wish on my worst enemy. But somehow Mama managed. Plenty of times soup was our main meal, but like a tiger Mama held on to the bag of money she was saving for Iz to go into business. That money often was on my mind. Why should Iz get it? What about the rest of us?

For a year that money was like a fire burning me up. While I took any job I could get, carrying bundles again, making infants' dresses at home, finishing, anything, I thought about that money.

That year I had my sixteenth birthday. Even Mama softened and said that she would buy me something that I wanted. What I wanted more than anything was to go to hear Caruso sing. Everywhere people were saying that his voice was like something from heaven, and I thought that before I died I would like to hear him. So I wouldn't have to go alone, Inez came with me. Together we took the trolley uptown to the opera house, and we bought the cheapest tickets we could get. We climbed and we climbed way up high in the balcony until I thought maybe we would land in heaven. But when he started to sing, it was like I was in heaven. For two, three hours, I don't know, I sat there like someone put a spell on me. Who cared about money, about layoffs, about adding another potato to the soup? *Oy*, such music. It was beautiful. I'll never forget it as long as I live.

But more than that. Mr. Caruso doesn't know it, but he turned my life around from back to front. At the opera house, Inez and I stared like two dummies, two Kuni Lemmels, at the fine ladies with their diamonds sparkling and their lace gowns and the gentlemen in their tall, silk hats. We had never been up close to such elegance. But it was the music more than anything else that gave me ideas.

Here we were in America, where anyone with a dollar could go to hear such beauty. And if you had more than a dollar you could buy the finest things in the world. I was no longer a girl, already a young woman. If I was ever going to have the fine things in America, I had better start right away.

When I got home I examined myself in the mirror. A beauty I wasn't, but also I wasn't so bad looking. Like Mama had said, my figure was developed so I went in and out in the right places. Esther often said she wished she had my eyes, they were so bright, and my complexion and hair were not bad. When he was in a good mood, Cousin Sam remarked that I made him wish he were younger and that I walked like a queen. So what? I was still a nobody. In this country four years, with my English pretty good, I could read everything—I never stopped taking books every Saturday from the library— but I wasn't making much more money than a green-horn.

As for marriage, I had to keep telling Mama not to bother me. The day after my birthday I was still inspired to do something with my life, thinking how I could go about it. I felt the fire in me burning so strong that if I didn't act pretty quick, it would flare up and die. Soon I would be old and empty like one of our candles with the wick burned out.

So then Mama started *hoking* me *a tchynic* I should let her invite Mr. Shapiro to come over. She picked the wrong time. "Leave me alone about Mr. Shapiro. Please, Mama, I am not interested."

"Interested you don't have to be," Mama said. "All I ask is you should be polite. You should at least talk to him. Who knows what fine, educated young man Mr. Shapiro has up his sleeve? You can at least listen."

"*I* know. He has no fine, educated young man who would want me. I'm a nobody. Besides, I don't want any man, educated or not. Look at Esther. Living here with her husband and baby in one room, and soon you'll see another baby on the way. What kind of a life has she got? Iz hasn't had a steady job since they got married. He's not a dumbbell, but you yourself are afraid to give him all your money to go into business for himself. You don't say it, but I know that's why you're holding back. For a girl like me, with nothing, Mr. Shapiro would only find another Iz. No, thank you. I don't want it."

"So what's so fine about your life?" Mama demanded, looking at me over her eyeglasses. "At least Esther won't be alone when she gets old. She'll have a husband and her children. A family is more than money. It's better to eat soup with a family than to eat roast chicken alone."

"First I want to get the roast chicken," I told her.

But how was I going to get it? I thought and I thought. I walked around the streets. By myself I went uptown where the garment business was growing and watched the men push the carts of clothes through the streets. Some people were making a lot of money. I wanted to be one of them. It was like I had to pluck out of myself the idea that I knew was someplace inside. Like you have to scratch a place that itches, I wanted my own business.

One day I went to see Cousin Sam when he came out of work. He was tired and wanted to go home, but I persuaded him he should come into a coffeehouse with me. "Don't laugh," I said to him, "don't right away say I'm *meshugge*. But how about you and Iz and me going into our own business?"

I spoke fast so he wouldn't interrupt. "I can make the samples. I know how. You're a first-rate cutter, and Iz and me and Mama too, we can all work on the machines. We can start small, and when we grow we'll hire girls for the machines."

Sam looked at me like I was a *meshuggeneh*. "Where do you think we're going to get the money to pay the rent? And what are you planning to make? Clothes out of paper? Maybe we would need money to buy material too, huh?"

"Mama has some money. She's been saving to start Iz in business. But I thought this would be better. Maybe you have a little money saved too? We wouldn't need much. We should make only children's dresses. Not so much material, not such different styles every season. Maybe only white dresses for graduation, for confirmation, for holidays. Even poor people buy such dresses. It's a steady business. Now so many Italian people, Irish people come to America, we would have plenty of customers."

Sam looked at me like he didn't know what to say. "Who gave you such an idea?" he asked.

"No one. I gave it to myself. You think it's good?"

"Not so bad. Not so dumb." He spoke like he was doing me a favor.

"For white dresses we don't need so many different styles. We don't need such a big stock of material. What we make should be good, but if we stick to one thing it's easier." I was still talking fast.

Sam pulled on his chin like he still had his beard there. "Not such a dumb idea," he repeated. "But I don't know. What do you want a business for? Better for you to have a husband and a family like your sister Esther. We start a business, and the next thing you'll get married."

"I don't think so. Besides, look in the shops and factories. The girls and women there are married. Even with a husband they need the money. Women work. If it's not in the factory, it's working on the machine at home."

"Well, I'll think about it. I'll give it a lot of thought," Sam said.

Me, I couldn't think of anything else. When I went to the store, I forgot what I needed to buy. Mama, with her sharp eye, soon noticed my mind was not where it should be. "What's the matter with you?" she asked. "You keeping something from me?" She smiled like she knew a secret. "You met some young man? What's the matter? You don't want to bring him home to meet your family?"

"Where do you think I would meet someone, on the street? I don't talk to strangers on the street."

"So why do you look so? Like you know something but are not saying?"

"Why can't she have a secret?" Inez asked. Inez, the baby, was getting more grown-up all the time. Twelve years old and already like a young lady. More and more, she kept to herself, aloof from the rest of the family. She had friends in school and was like a one hundred percent American. Hardly ever she brought anyone home, and I suspected she was ashamed of our poor, crowded apartment. I couldn't blame her. There was not even place for her friends to sit in our kitchen. We had no parlor, and she couldn't very well take them into the bedroom, with no place to turn around either. What I worried about was that not all her friends were Jewish girls and boys. Sometimes I saw her on the street with young people I didn't think were Jewish. It was not a crime to have Gentile friends, but God forbid she should fall in love with a Gentile boy. That would be trouble.

Sundays she was out all the time. Sometimes she and her friends went all the way up to Central Park to ice skate, to walk, I don't know what. Even Saturdays she did not keep the Sabbath, but rode in trolley cars. I kept her secret from Mama and did not let on that I myself knew. I prayed that she did nothing worse. I could not forget that I myself had once eaten pork, so how could I question her? With Inez we were all lenient, and maybe too much so.

But it was not Inez who was on my mind those days. I was impatient to see Sam again, yet I made myself wait for a week. Better not to rush, better not to let him think I was in such a hurry.

But when I went to his place, he wasn't there. I learned there had been a walkout because the bosses wouldn't sign with the union, and they had hired new greenhorns who didn't know from the union. So Sam was out of a job. Maybe his misfortune could be my luck. Right away, I went to his house. Like I thought, he was in a terrible slump, and I think if I had said, "Let's go buy the Brooklyn Bridge," he would have agreed.

"Why not?" Sam said. "In this cutthroat business it's dog eat dog. The needle trade. If a girl puts a needle through her finger, nobody stops to help. She's got to get herself a new needle yet. If I could find another trade, I'd be happy. But if I have to stay in this to feed my family, just as well to be my own boss. May the swine choke on their *knishes*." He was referring to his old bosses, and he spat to get even the mention of them out of his mouth.

Back home, Mama didn't know what to think. First she said, "*Oy*, a crazy girl. Who do you think you are? Such ideas you get in your head. A business of your own yet. You think you're Mr. Goodman, you can run a factory? Better you should learn to make *gefilte* fish." She was referring to Jacob Goodman, the big cloak-and-suit man.

"Mama, we're not going to start with a big factory. Just a little operation. Why do we need to work for someone to sell to a jobber? We can sell to the same jobber ourselves."

After she settled down, she said, "A crazy idea. But for Iz maybe it's the best thing, and if Sam thinks it's good. . . ."

Iz didn't have to think twice. Right away he was making big money, moving into their own apartment, talking about buying one of those horseless carriages like he was a millionaire.

Only about the carriage Esther got excited. "Iz, if you make a million dollars, promise me you won't buy one of those things. Think of me and our Nathan. A widow I don't want to be. For a million dollars I wouldn't go into such a contraption."

So right away they had a quarrel about an automobile when we were still eating potato-and-barley soup. And Inez had to put her two cents in.

"I think they're wonderful," she said. "One of these days I'm going to go for a ride in one. It would be exciting. I'll get one of those cute hats with a long veil. . . ."

"Nothing doing," Mama screamed. "Bad enough to see one on the street, scaring the horses, frightening the children. Don't you dare go near one. *Oy, oy,* it's too much for an old woman to have such daughters."

I had to laugh at them all. But I knew Mama well. To help Iz was like doing something for Nathan, her beloved grandson, and soon she would let go of her bag of money.

8

So that was how we got started. Finkelstein (that was Sam, whose name he said had to go first, and who was I to argue with the king cutter?), Solomon, and Ginsberg. How we worked! We slaved from early in the morning until late at night. On Sixteenth Street we rented a small place, and first I made a sample line of infants' dresses. Beautiful white dresses with ribbons and lace for a *bris* or a baptism. Iz and Mama worked on the machines, and Sam, too, when he was through cutting. (He complained it was not right for a cutter, but he did it anyhow.)

I made just a few samples at first, maybe half a dozen, a dozen. Sam knew a jobber, and he brought him over to see what we had. My heart was in my mouth. Mr. Goldberg, a big man with a big smile and plenty of jokes. He looked, he turned the little dresses inside out, like maybe he'd find a mistake in our workmanship or a piece of gold. But he gave an order for a dozen of one dress and two dozen of another. Three dozen dresses, our first order.

Sam said, "From this we'll never get rich."

But I said, "Wait, don't be impatient. We got to start somewhere."

In a week Mr. Goldberg came back with another order, this time for more. Then Sam went out to sell and more orders came in.

So through the season we rushed, rushed to get out the orders.

As time went by, the business was going well, but still we were all living together in the crowded apartment. One evening I said to Esther, "Don't you think you and Iz should move." Already little Nathan, God bless him, was no longer in the crib all day. He was all over the place. And Esther was going to have another child.

"Iz says to wait," Esther said. Her face was pale and drawn from her morning sickness. "He's nervous. He says the business is all right now, but how does he know it will last?"

"*Oy*, Iz. How do I know the sun will rise tomorrow? Maybe not, but you've got to believe. He'll die an old man still worrying whether the business will make good."

Esther leaned against me. "Not everyone's like you, Rachel. You've got spirit, confidence. You should have been a man."

That got me angry. "Why a man? A woman can't have spirit? The men are *shlemiels,* most of them, anyway. Jewish women are strong, they work hard, they keep the family together. Don't tell me I should be a man. Thank God I'm a woman."

"That's what you say now. Wait till you get married and you have to please a man, take care of the children. Always you have to be patient, even when the husband isn't exactly perfect."

"If I ever have a husband, he'll have to take me the way I am. I'll never live just to please him." I held Esther to me. I wished I could give her some of what she called my spirit. I knew she wasn't altogether happy. Iz was a good man, but he gave in to his moods. I think he was disappointed so far in his life and was seldom cheerful. For company, Esther had to laugh and joke with Mama and me, not with her husband. Maybe that was why she was not so anxious to move.

One day, a fine, sunny day, I was walking home from work when I passed a young woman, about my age, on the sidewalk. She stared at me and I stared at her. She walked with her head up like she felt she was somebody. Stylish looking, but not in a fancy way. A working girl who knew how to dress. After we kept looking at each other like one of us should say something, she turned to me. "I think I know you," she said in good English with an Irish accent.

Then I remembered. "You're the girl on the boat. You were crying because they took your bird away."

"Yes, yes." Her blue eyes shone in the sunlight.

Like we were long-lost sisters, we hugged and walked on together.

That day marked the beginning of my friendship with Eileen O'Brien. We were like twins. Everything we did together. She worked in a shirtwaist factory, the biggest, but we planned that someday, when I had a big place, she would be the forelady for Finklestein, Solomon, and Ginsberg. Such dreams we had. Mama didn't like I was such close friends with a Gentile girl, but I told her, "Don't worry. Eileen I can't marry, and her boyfriends, if she has any, I don't see."

That wasn't exactly the truth. She did have a boyfriend, and I did meet him. A fine-looking Irish boy, a bricklayer, who all the time teased me that he would introduce me to a rich *goy*. Mama didn't know, but often on a Sunday the three of us had good times together. We rode on the ferry, and once we went to Coney Island and walked on the boardwalk. They ate kosher sandwiches with me, and, God forgive me, persuaded me to taste a clam. How they laughed when I couldn't swallow it and finally had to spit it out. I loved Eileen like my own sister. Such a cheerful disposition, not melancholy like so many of us Jews are. Only in America, I thought, could I have such a friend of a different faith.

But I was ashamed, too, that I had so much pleasure outside of our house. My family still was everything to me, but our home was gloomy. Only little Nathan was laughing and cheerful. Iz was complaining but afraid to move. Esther was not feeling well with her pregnancy, and Mama had always something to worry about. The meat was tough, the butcher robbed her, Esther wasn't eating enough, Inez put powder on her face, next it would be rouge, and if nothing else, she worried about the business. Without Eileen and her Shawn, my life would have been drab. I began to understand better why Inez was always out with her friends.

Often we sat late in a coffeehouse, drinking tea, talking about our hopes. Eileen was the one who said to me, "Someday you'll be a rich lady, while I'm married to a bricklayer. You'll forget all about me."

"Never," I told her. "I'll never forget you. But I do want to be rich. Do you think that's very sinful? It isn't that I crave money so much. I want my family to have all the fine things to be had in America. More, I want the accomplishment. I want to succeed, to have respect, to have something I can be proud of. I like what I do. I get pleasure out of thinking up new styles, of seeing the dresses go from something in my head to something a little girl will wear and get pleasure out of. I like to see the orders pile up." I had never talked to anyone like this before. I was worried my friend would think I was too ambitious, and I asked her.

Eileen shook her head. "I don't think so. I think it's wonderful to have something you feel like that about. And to have a talent. You will succeed because you're smart and you have the push to do it. I admire you very much."

Her words encouraged me. Our business was not all uphill, however. Among my samples there sometimes was a lemon or two, a dress that nobody wanted. That hurt me. And Sam would look at me like I was a nothing, a fool. And even with the good sellers, there were plenty of headaches. Maybe we get a big order and then can't get the material in time to fill it. Or I would turn out a beautiful dress, and before I knew it every one on the street would be copying my style. Like Sam said, it was dog eat dog.

But yet, with my new friends, for the first time since we had come to America, I could say I was enjoying myself. But the happy time did not continue.

One day in March I came out of work and decided to walk home. As I came downtown near Washington Place there were crowds of people and so much excitement on the street. People talked in low voices, looking frightened. I thought, Was someone murdered?

"What happened?" I asked an old woman with a shawl around her head.

"A big fire. Terrible. So many girls burned. Someone said hundreds are dead."

Then I recognized the smell of burning in the air. A couple of blocks down I could see the ladders and firemen and part of a building still smoking. My heart dropped.

"Where was the fire?" I asked near to fainting, because already I knew the answer: where my friend Eileen worked.

The woman told me, and I was right. "Three floors they say burned," she said. "Some jumped out of the windows, seven flights up. Not even enough coffins for them, I heard."

I turned away. I didn't want to hear more. The woman looked like she didn't know where she was, and I thought maybe she had a daughter in the fire. I had no heart to speak.

Eileen perhaps was saved, I told myself. But how to find out? Where Shawn lived, I didn't know, or where he worked. I was sick with worry. Eileen lived with her family in an apartment over her father's bar, but I was afraid to go there. If, God forbid, she was dead, maybe a stranger wouldn't be so welcome at this time.

But to go home without knowing was impossible too. I walked and walked. For blocks I could smell the smoke and hear the talk of the fire on the streets. It was the worst tragedy that had happened in the needle trade. I could not walk all night, and soon Mama would worry herself sick.

Finally I couldn't stand not knowing anymore, so I went to the bar. Now and then, when she had the time, she helped her father serve the beer there. When I got to it my heart sank. The door was closed, it was all dark, and I knew that was no good.

I went upstairs to where the family lived and stood

outside the door. After a minute or two I got up my courage to knock. Eileen's brother, even at such a time, was polite enough to apologize for not asking me in. I knew by his face immediately the terrible news. "We are waiting for her body to be brought to us," he said. "Come back tomorrow if you care to pay your respects."

"I care," I told him, nodding my head. I did not want to add my tears to his sorrow. Quickly I turned away.

Iz had already brought the terrible news home, and I told them about Eileen. I had no place to go to be alone with my sorrow. In my house, they all were sorry and said how terrible it was, but everything was as usual. Mama had supper on the table; Nathan, God bless him, was playing. I could not eat, and I could not sleep either. I thought, What kind of God killed all those girls who had done no wrong? Why, why should such a thing happen?

I did not go to work the next day. I told Iz they would have to get along without me and went instead to Eileen's apartment. Right away I could see it was a place of mourning, with the front door draped in black. On the street people were talking about the fire and about Eileen. They had known her since she was a little girl. I kept remembering, too, when first I saw her. Such a sweet face she had.

I felt strange with no familiar Jewish faces around me, but the people were kind. Although I knew my way, they showed me where to go upstairs.

The door was open, but I stood in the hallway. I was too shy to go in with so many strangers. The apartment looked like maybe a party was going on. I could smell the beer, and it was hard to know if people were crying or singing. Fortunately, God bless him, Shawn saw me and came to the door to greet me. He put his arms around me, and then I cried. The tears flowed like from a river. Shawn cried with me. A big strong man, he cried pitifully, like a baby. Together we stood holding on to each other, wanting to give comfort and to get it. Maybe we did. Finally we quieted down, and Shawn lifted up my face and looked at me. "Eileen loved you," he said.

"I loved her, too. My only friend. Like a sister to me." I looked at the coffin in the middle of the room, draped around with flowers.

Shawn's face turned harsh. "She was badly burned, Rachel. I'll never forgive them, never, never."

Again I had to fight back the tears. Why, I asked myself again, why should such a thing have to happen in the great United States?

Shawn led me over to Eileen's mother. Like an older Eileen she looked—the same sweet face, the same blue eyes. She took me in her arms, too. "Eileen talked about you. She said you were smart. Someday you were going to be rich, and she was going to work for you. My Eileen. . . ." She held my hand tightly in hers, and I sat beside her.

I could hear the talk around me, especially from the men. They said the fire didn't have to happen. No one cared about the workers, they said. "Those girls worked in a firetrap. No exit, no proper fire escape," one man said.

"The company was afraid of the union," another

man answered. "For two years the doors to the stairs were locked to keep the union organizers from getting in. A crime, a terrible crime."

If what they said was true, the factory owners were murderers. I wanted to ask more questions: how the fire started, were the people responsible going to be punished? But I sat quietly as I didn't think it was proper to ask.

I didn't stay too long. To be with Eileen's family and so many strangers, but without my friend there to talk with me, made me want to cry.

Out in the fresh air, I walked around until I came to a little park where I could sit down and rest. The thoughts in my head were going round and round. The talk I had heard upset me because none of it was going to bring Eileen or all the other dead girls back to life. But I kept wondering whether I was doing the right thing to have a business of my own. The talk had also been that now the union would get stronger, it would change the conditions for the workers in the factories. Maybe I was doing the wrong thing. Maybe I should be on the other side, should join the union and help to right these wrongs.

The thought would not go away from me, and I wished I had someone to talk to. I was an uneducated girl, and it was hard for me to know what was right and what was wrong. But even someone uneducated has to figure things out, and I figured this way. To give up the business would be unfair to Sam and Iz since, after all, I was the one who persuaded them to go into it. And also, what would happen to Mama and Inez, and even Esther and Iz and Nathan and the new baby when it arrived? Better we make a success of it so Inez can get a good education—my dream was that she should become a teacher—and Nathan, too. He should someday be a lawyer.

Besides, the truth was that deep in my heart I knew I did not want to be another girl tied to the machine. The union would have to get along without me. I wanted something of my own; I wanted to create a business I could be proud of, so that when I walked down the street people would say, "There goes Rachel Ginsberg, a fine lady." I didn't mind the hard work. Even the ups and downs were not so bad, because with them came excitement. It was exciting when an order came in, exciting when I made a sample so beautiful I wanted to take a picture of it, exciting to see the pretty dresses finished and imagine a happy little girl getting one of them. Also, I had learned to go uptown to the big stores to see what they were showing so I would get ideas for new styles. I enjoyed walking around the shops like a fine lady.

But one thing I made up my mind about. If ever we did have a real factory and the union wanted to come in, I would not stand in the way. If the girls working for me wanted the union, and the leaders seemed like honest people, I would not forget today or forget my friend Eileen. I would not be a murderer and fight to keep the union out. In business you had to make adjustments, to think only of making money could be a curse.

In our small business—even without the union—we had plenty of problems. Plenty of heartache. Between Iz and Sam there were sometimes rifts. Sam was more daring; always he wanted something new and different. Iz was more cautious. If we had a dress that went well, he wanted to make the same one, maybe just a little different, the next year. Add a bow or a ruffle here or there. I agreed more with Sam and was not afraid to take a chance, but I worried Iz should get insulted.

After the terrible fire, I turned back to my books. With Eileen and Shawn there had not been so much time to read, but now I thought I did not want to make any more friends. To lose such a friend hurts so much that I decided better to stick to the books. They would be my friends. The lady in the library was very kind and helped to pick out worthwhile books to read. I read more of Charles Dickens and some of George Eliot. When the librarian told me George Eliot was a lady, I was more interested than ever. Such a wonderful writer, and for a woman to write so much was beautiful. Also I read Rudyard Kipling, beautiful stories about India, and funny short stories by O. Henry. Everything she gave me I read—poems, writings about nature, a book about the American revolution, stories by Mark Twain, and a book called *Uncle Tom's Cabin*. Mama said I would go blind from reading, but to me it was better than thinking about my friend and all those girls burned in a fire. It was a shame that in such a fine country some people cared more about getting rich than they did for human life.

9

When trouble comes, it does not come alone. Mama said it was not meant for Jews to be happy, but I say that is a *bobbe-myseh*. Where does it say that? Not in the Talmud, not in the Jewish laws. What did the Jews ever do that they should be picked out special not to be happy? Is it something to be proud of, a special honor, that we Jews should suffer?

The trouble began when Esther went into labor. Again Mary the midwife came, and right away she said the baby was not in the right position. Iz ran to get a doctor, but the doctor, a young man who looked more scared than Iz, could do from nothing. Poor Esther. She didn't want to scream with Nathan in the house, but she couldn't help it. Finally somehow the baby got born, a tiny little thing, but he lived only a few hours.

For Esther there was no consolation. Mild Esther, like a wild woman she was. She tore at her hair, she wailed; no one, not Iz, not Mama, not me, could quiet her. A house of mourning we had. Mama covered the mirror and made a rip in our clothes, and after the poor little thing was buried we sat *shivah*. Every morning and evening for the seven days a *minyan* came, but after three days Iz and I went to our business for a while. Mama carried on that we were not Jews to go to work, that we were breaking her heart, but I told her to stay home a whole week would hurt the living, and the dead no one could bring back. Already it was May, and the fall line we had to get out. If not, we would lose the whole season.

The business prospered. By another year, we hired some Italian girls to work on the machines. Nice girls who did their work and didn't waste their time talking. But even as the months passed, my heart was still sad from losing Eileen and also Esther's baby. Such pain you don't get over one, two, three.

But life is such that time goes by. It seemed that one day I was eighteen and the next twenty. Twenty years old. An old maid, Mama teased me. She was almost crazy that I wouldn't let her bring Mr. Shapiro to the house. Maybe I was going to be an old maid. That didn't appeal to me, but neither did Mr. Shapiro. Whatever would be, would be.

But who knows from one day to the next what will happen? You wake up in the morning, wash yourself, eat your breakfast, and expect this day will be like any other day. No different. But all of a sudden something can happen you never expected. That's the way it was when I met Abe Levine.

The first time I saw him I hardly remember. He was another salesman, coming to peddle his silk. Mainly Sam saw the salesmen, since the cutter knew best if the material would work good or not. So I paid no attention to Abe Levine; I didn't care if he had red hair or green hair. A salesman was a salesman. I cared about what he had to sell, not if he smiled or not. He should give me a good price, and his jokes he could leave at home.

But with Abe Levine it was different. How many times he'd been in before, I didn't count. One day Sam called me over. I'm looking at some crepe de chine, and all of a sudden Abe said to me, "You like to listen to music?"

Maybe he heard something I didn't hear. I said, "Music? You hearing music?"

Abe Levine laughed, like I was a funny lady on the vaudeville stage. "No, I don't hear any music. I have a couple of tickets for a concert, and I thought maybe you'd like to go with me. Would you?"

Then I looked at him. Not bad looking. Red hair and a mustache that you could make from it a whisk broom. Pink cheeks and no gold teeth. A good build, not scrawny like some men. But I'm not so anxious. If I went with him to a concert, maybe he'd expect we should buy more goods from him. To be obligated to a salesman, I thought, was not a smart idea.

All this was going through my head while he looked at me and I looked at the material.

Abe Levine was not a dumbbell. Right away he figured out what I was thinking. "This has nothing to do with business," he said. "Sure I'd like to get an order, but if you don't need what I've got, that's okay. I'd still like you to come to the concert with me."

Such a beautiful smile he had. White teeth, like they were polished every day. The thoughts didn't count anymore; my heart was doing the thinking. Before I knew it I said yes.

"Can I pick you up here when you finish work? We can have a bite to eat and go to the concert?"

"Tonight, you mean?" I was thinking my hair wasn't washed and I was wearing an old blouse.

"Yes. Anything wrong with that?"

"I don't know. I guess not."

"All right. I'll meet you here at six o'clock."

He didn't even wait for Sam to give him an order. In a minute he disappeared as if he didn't want to give me a chance to change my mind. Or maybe, I thought with a smile, he was nervous same as I was.

"What happened to Levine?" Sam asked. "I wanted to give him an order."

"He left."

"What's the matter? You had an argument with him?"

"No. He'll be back. He'll be back at six o'clock."

Sam gave me a funny look, but I pretended to be busy with my sample.

Such a day I never would want to live again. This was the first time in my life a man invited me anywhere. I was afraid to tell Sam, to tell Iz. Afraid they would stop me. Who was Abe Levine? I knew nothing about him. Concert, shmoncert, did I know where he was taking me? But the more I was frightened, the more I made up my mind I wanted to go. From here to there I went back and forth. Why should I think he was no good? A man with such a beautiful smile, what harm could he do me? But in the *Forward* there were stories of plenty of harm young women could get from strange men. But was Abe Levine a stranger? I'm telling you, you could go *meshugge* from what went on in my head all day.

But I had to tell Iz, or Mama would be worried sick that I didn't come home. Come near six o'clock I was close to dying. To go out with a young man alone, with no one else along, with no proper introduction, that was bad enough. But on top of that not to be dressed my best, to be wearing an old *shmatte*, I should have my head examined.

"Iz, I'm not going home with you tonight," I said.

"I can find my way alone. Where are you going?"

"Tell Mama I'm meeting a friend." That wasn't a lie. Iz gave me a look. "What kind of a friend?"

"A friend. What do you mean, what kind? A person. A friend I met. A girl can't have a friend?"

Still he was looking at me funny, but since it was time to go home, no more questions. For a minute I thought, Should I be insulted? Iz wasn't thinking for a second that maybe I could have a man friend.

Iz left. Always in a hurry to leave early anyhow. But Sam kept finding more things to do until I wanted to push him out the door. To go over the books, to measure out some material. God knows what else he would find to delay him. "I thought you said Abe Levine was coming back at six," he said.

"He said some such thing. Maybe he changed his mind."

But six o'clock sharp Abe Levine walked in. Sam greeted him and talked like it was eight o'clock in the morning instead of time to go home. I stood around like a dummy, not knowing what to do. Then Sam said to me, "What are you waiting for?"

Before I could answer Mr. Levine said, "She's going to a concert with me."

Sam looked at him, and he looked at me. Then he smiled, like all of a sudden he caught someone doing something not so nice. A smile I didn't like. "Oh, so you two are going out together. Does your mother know, Rachel?"

His head should turn into a turnip with his questions.

"We just decided this morning," I said. "Besides, I don't consult my mother on my appointments, thank you."

Mr. Busybody laughed. I could have smacked him.

"Maybe you need a secretary for your appointments. So, have a good time," he said. "What do I care?"

"No one asked you to care," I told him and turned away.

Mr. Levine said, "We'd better get going or we'll be late." So we left with Mr. Wise-guy Sam staring after us.

Out on the street, Mr. Levine offered me his arm, which I took like I'd seen the ladies on Fifth Avenue do. I thought even in my everyday clothes I was a true American lady walking on the street with a gentleman. Not like in the old country, where always a young couple had to be watched, where a meeting together had to be arranged by the elders. I was no longer afraid. I felt free like a bird.

Mr. Levine treated me like I was made of china. Around the puddles he walked me—I mustn't get my feet wet, he said. He should have known all the puddles that had wet my feet in my lifetime.

We walked a few blocks, and he asked me if I'm tired. Would I like to eat? That day I was too nervous to eat the lunch Mama gave me, so I'd had no food since six o'clock in the morning. Yes, I was hungry. "I don't mind," I said. He took me into a restaurant I had passed often but had not dared to go into, it looked so fancy.

He asked me if I cared for a glass of wine. I was ashamed to tell him it might make me dizzy, so I said again I wouldn't mind. We drank wine, and he ordered a dinner from soup to nuts. The food was good, but I left a little on my plate so he wouldn't think I was starving from not eating all day.

Mr. Levine was pretty good at conversation. It was a

blessing for me that I didn't have to talk much. To listen to him was a pleasure.

He told me he lived in Paterson, New Jersey, and he had worked in the mill before he became a salesman. He lived with his married brother, who had four children and a nagging wife. "I want a home of my own," he said, and he looked at me in a way that made me nervous all over again. "You should know from the beginning that marriage is very much on my mind," he said.

From the beginning of what, I thought. What was on his mind did not have to be on my mind. "Why aren't you married then?" I asked. "It's not such a hardship to find a rabbi to perform a ceremony."

Mr. Levine laughed. "That's not the problem. It's to find the right person to marry."

"I can give you the name of a *shadchen*. He can help you."

"That's not what I want. I don't believe in match-makers. I want to marry for love."

"But you talk like you want to buy a parcel of goods. You want to get married; you want to find the right person. But love doesn't come that way. It's not something you make up your mind to, like you want to buy a new suit. Love comes without looking for it, I think."

"Maybe it has already come to me," he said. "What would you think of that?"

"I think then you had better find a rabbi in a hurry," I told him.

Fortunately, our dinner was over, and the conversation had to come to an end. From such a conversation I didn't know what to think. Maybe Mr. Levine was so unhappy in his house he needed someone to tell his troubles to. But why did he pick on me? On his face there was a question, as if I should have an answer. But with such a stranger I was timid. Better to have jokes than a serious conversation.

The music was beautiful. A violin player like I never heard. With such sweet music I forgot all my troubles and thought only how beautiful life was. Mr. Levine was a musical man, I could tell by his face. Quiet, like he was feeling every note from the music. Refined.

After the concert he asked me again would I care to have something to eat or drink, but this time I thought no, better I go home. Mama will be worrying herself sick where I am by this time. Mr. Levine took me to my door, and when we shook hands good-night he held my hand and said, "It was a beautiful evening, and I hope we can repeat it soon. May I ask you out again?"

Not to appear too anxious, I said, "If I have no other engagement, it would be nice if you care to."

"I care to very much," he said, and he looked me in the eyes with a look that made me feel light-headed. I wondered whether he looked that way at many girls. Why should I care? He was nothing to me, another salesman maybe being nice to get a big order. But in my heart I hoped that was not so.

As I expected, Mama was pretty near fainting when I came upstairs. "You will kill me," she cried. "Better I should drop dead this minute than have a daughter go chasing around all night, God knows where, without a word, without a permission. That I should live to have a bum for a daughter! What have I done to deserve such a punishment? I've slaved to the bone to bring you up a good, respectable girl. *Oy vay iz mir*, God should forgive me where I've done wrong. . . ."

She carried on like already I was a tramp, a woman from the streets. "Mama, listen to me. Calm down, you'll give yourself a heart attack for no reason. I'm a grown woman with my own business, twenty years old, I don't need your permission to go out in the evening. We're living in America, in the twentieth century, no longer back in the eighties and nineties. I earn my own money; I've got a right to do what I want. And besides, what I did wasn't bad."

"So, because you earn a living you got a right to punish me? To tear out my heart? What do I care that you got a business? I spit on your business. Better you stay home like a decent girl, live respectable with a husband and a family, than to run around all night with a bum."

"I wasn't running around with a bum," I screamed. "Will you listen to me?"

At last I got her to calm down so I could tell her about the dinner and the concert, and tell her about Mr. Levine. A lot of good it did. All over again she got excited. Who was Mr. Levine? What did she know from a Mr. Levine? A nice man would come to the house and meet the mother before he took a girl out. I should be ashamed to talk to her about a Mr. Levine. She didn't want to know about him.

It was no use arguing anymore, so I told her I wanted to go to sleep. In my bed, my heart was heavy, but also I had a feeling that even though there would be trouble ahead, it might be good trouble. A trouble that was not the sad kind, but maybe something that would make me happy.

I was a foolish girl. Afterward, every day at work, I had one eye on the door, waiting for Mr. Levine to make his appearance. I went from hot to cold, from cold to hot. One minute I would think, Maybe Mr. Levine got hit by a horse, maybe by one of those automobiles. He could be in a hospital and I wouldn't know. Then when a day passed and no Mr. Levine, I thought Mama was right. He *is* a bum, no good, I shouldn't give him a second thought. Why should I eat my heart out because a Mr. Levine doesn't come around? But then I thought of how he looked at me when he said goodnight, and again my heart would melt like butter. If only I had been wearing my best dress. Why should Mr. Levine want to see again a girl who went out in such *shmattes*?

"What's the matter with you?" Sam asked on Friday, the end of the week. "You sit around like a sick cow. You not feeling well?"

"Nothing's the matter. I feel fine," I told him. But it wasn't the truth. My heart was sick.

Saturday night Inez was going out with her friends. Esther and Iz went to visit a cousin of Iz's. Mama and I stayed home with Nathan. A hundred times I had done this before, happy to read my book, to drink a cup of tea with Mama. But that Saturday night I could not sit still. I read one page a dozen times and at the end didn't know what I'd read. What girl was Mr. Levine taking out tonight? I didn't have to close my eyes to see him walking down the street with a fancy girl on his arm. Or maybe sitting in a café looking into her eyes, like he had looked into mine.

Again I went from hot to cold. Why should I care about Mr. Levine? I had my business, someday it would be a big factory, and Mr. Levine would say that once he had known Rachel Ginsberg. My name would be known all over East New York. I would give money to the Jewish charities. Maybe a glass window to a synagogue. An important woman, Rachel Ginsberg. Who needed a nobody silk salesman from Paterson, New Jersey?

But then my heart felt cut, like with a knife, because just a businesswoman I wasn't. I was a girl ashamed before her own mother that she had no man to admire her, to make her feel the way she did with Mr. Levine. To be sitting home with her mother the rest of her life was not an appetizing thought. Mama didn't say a word, but with her eyes she was pleading, My poor Rachel, my stubborn Rachel, please, let me bring Mr. Shapiro over to introduce you. Why sit here with an old woman when you can have a husband?

But it wasn't any husband I was thinking of. My thoughts were on a man with bright eyes and red hair, with a body that walked straight and strong. To have such a man ask you out once and never come back was a hurt worse than never to be asked at all.

10

By Sunday afternoon thinking of Mr. Abe Levine was a sickness with me, a sickness no doctor could cure. To keep busy, I thought, was the best medicine. I washed clothes that were clean, I swept the floor that had no dirt, I looked for holes to mend. All *fartootst* I was, like a chicken without a head.

Poor Mama. She didn't know what to make of me. "What's the matter, you can't sit still? All of a sudden you don't like how I keep the house? It's not good enough for her highness?"

"It's not that, Mama. I'm a little nervous."

"Nervous. Sure you're nervous. A young girl who doesn't let her mother introduce her is nervous. Tonight I'm going to see Mr. Shapiro. He can cure you."

"Mr. Shapiro, Mr. Shapiro. Don't *hok* me *a tchynik* with Mr. Shapiro."

I was in my oldest dress with my hair tied up in a scarf when there was a knock on the door. Inez answered it. Standing there was Mr. Levine.

I was near to fainting. "How do you do?" says he. "I was in the neighborhood, and I thought you wouldn't mind if I stopped by to say hello."

I stared at him like a dummy.

"Mama, this is Mr. Levine," I said, when I could talk.

"Hello," Mama said, cold like ice.

I introduced him to Inez and Esther. Iz wasn't there.

Little Nathan, God bless him, ran over to Mr. Levine and showed him a toy he was playing with. Mr. Levine bent down and said a few words to him. Mama softened a little. "We were not expecting company," she said, "but maybe you would care for a cup of tea."

"That would be very nice," said Mr. Levine.

So while Mama fixed the tea, I ran into my room and pulled the scarf from my head and arranged my hair. To change my dress would have been too noticeable.

Esther excused herself and went into her room, and Inez put on her jacket and said she was going out for a walk. That left Mama and me with Mr. Levine. Not a good prospect for a conversation. Mama's face was not what I could call encouraging. "You live in this neighborhood?" she asked, knowing well that he did not.

"No. I live in Paterson. Paterson, New Jersey."

"But you come here to go for a walk. No place to walk in Paterson, New Jersey?"

Mr. Levine laughed. "I had some business to do here."

Mama looked at him over her eyeglasses. "What kind of business do you do?"

"I'm a salesman. A silk salesman. I have some customers around here."

Mama looked like she was thinking hard. "You left your sample case on the street maybe?"

Mr. Levine looked at me and then at Mama. "All right. So I didn't have business in the neighborhood. I came to see your daughter, Miss Ginsberg." He did not speak like he was sorry for anything, but more like he was doing Mama the honor of telling her the truth.

He had a smile on his face as if he was laughing a little at Mama.

"So, *nu*, you see her," Mama said.

That remark Mr. Levine did not like. "If I'm not welcome here, I'll leave." But he sat like he was glued to his seat.

"You are welcome here," I said. Enough was enough. I didn't need such remarks from Mama, and Mr. Levine did not need insults. "Have more tea." I filled his cup again. Mama was looking innocent like a baby.

But with her questions she did not stop. He had to tell her that he lived with his brother and sister-in-law, that he had a father in Philadelphia. Also his father was a tailor, and he came from Minsk with his father and brother when he was eight, nine years old. His mother died in the old country.

"You never been married?" Mama asked. "Maybe a wife was too much money? Cheaper to live with your brother."

"Not exactly," Mr. Levine said. "Maybe I didn't find the right girl."

"Ah, the right girl," Mama said, after him. "A rich girl you're looking for?"

Mr. Levine laughed. He looked like he was playing a game with Mama and enjoying it. "What would I want with a rich girl, Mrs. Ginsberg? A rich girl wants fancy clothes, a fine house, servants. I'm a simple man with simple habits. A good house, good food, nice music—I like such things. But to support a rich wife, I am not interested."

For a moment Mama looked approving, but as if she didn't want anyone to notice. Again her face showed no expression. "May I ask what are you interested in?" She was so polite.

Mr. Levine leaned forward. "I am interested in happiness. I believe in marriage for love. I want a wife who will be a companion, not be a fool. I like a lively woman with a mind." He looked over at me in a way I thought he should not look in front of Mama. In my breast my heart turned over.

"You go to *shul*?" Mama asked.

"I won't lie to you. Sometimes I go. Not every Friday night. I'm a good Jew, but to be a good Jew is more important all week, not just on the Sabbath."

Mama had no answer for that. I sighed with relief because maybe the game was over and no one had won and no one had lost. What was important for me was Mr. Levine sitting in my kitchen, drinking tea. In his eyes I saw again what I had seen sitting in the restaurant. It should just stay that way, with no one rocking the boat.

But Mama kept on with her picking, like when she picked over the vegetables to make the soup. Maybe she'd find a worm. "A silk salesman makes good money?"

"Depends. When the season is good, everyone makes good money. When it's not so good, it's the same for me, too."

"So then you go hungry?"

"I don't go hungry, Mrs. Ginsberg."

"*Alevai*, you shouldn't go hungry," Mama said, with a look like she knew the game, too.

I did not care for the conversation, however. "You go to many concerts?" I asked to change the subject.

"I like music very much. Also I like shows. Would you care to go to see Jacob Adler with me next week?"

"Jacob Adler?" Mama was impressed. "You know Jacob Adler?"

Mr. Levine laughed. "No. I meant to go see him in the theater. I would like to get tickets."

"Mmph. You got money to spend to go see shows?"

"Mama, if Mr. Levine wants to see a show, that's his business." I could not keep my mouth shut forever.

"If he wants to take my daughter, that's my business," Mama said, high and mighty.

"But not how I spend my money." His voice was sweet like a bird. His eyes, not so sweet. Mr. Levine was no fool.

"I've never been to a show," I said.

Mama gave me a look saying don't be a *shlemiel* in front of him. But I didn't care. He should know from the beginning I was a plain Jewish girl. Why should I put on airs?

"Then it's high time to go, isn't it?" Like Mama wasn't there, he gave me another look.

"It would be very nice." I looked at him, too, right past Mama.

"I'll see what night I can get tickets, and I'll stop by the shop and tell you." Mr. Levine stood up. "Thank you for the tea. It was a pleasure to meet you, Mrs. Ginsberg." He bowed to Mama and to me and took his leave.

The minute the door was closed, Esther flew out of her room. "A *shayner* young man. Where did you find him? You never told me. Secrets you're keeping from me. *Oy*, my baby sister. . . . "

She hugged me like she hadn't seen me half an hour before. "Just a salesman who comes to the shop." A shrug to show he meant nothing to me, but my heart was going thump like a hammer.

You had to get up early in the morning to fool Mama and Esther. They looked at me as if they were examining a piece of goods. Esther laughed, but Mama wasn't so happy. She was looking down her nose. "A silk salesman. Why should anyone get excited over a silk salesman? Maybe you need a college education to cut a *shmatte* of silk?"

"Mama, he likes concerts. He knows about Jacob Adler." Esther spoke up for me. That she had not missed a word was a foregone conclusion.

"Such foolishness you talk. Will Jacob Adler pay the grocery bill? A violin maybe will buy the meat. A doctor, a lawyer has a future, but a silk salesman? All his life he'll peddle his piece goods."

Esther turned away. What she was thinking I felt in my heart. For Esther it was already too late. Mama's heartache for her was a hole in her breast, so now her dream was for me. For me now Mama wanted the best. An educated man, a professional, a who-knows-what, a *shayner mensh*. What did she care that his eyes were blue and a look from him made me shake like a cup of jelly. I was already worrying how soon he would come to tell me he had the tickets. Would he come for sure? And what would I wear? Already I knew that every day in the shop my eyes would be glued to the door, every day I would have to wear my blouse with the blue embroidery. I knew with a new ache that I could refuse Mr. Levine nothing. I felt sad for Mama.

I could understand what she wanted. But if Mr. Levine was a peddler on the street picking up rags, Mama could not have changed my heart. I was in love.

I consoled myself with the thought that Mama still had Inez. Bright, pretty Inez. Maybe for her Mama's dreams would come true, and a rich doctor or lawyer would come into our family.

11

"I should have a hat," I said to Esther the following Monday night.

"He came with the tickets?" She was as happy as if she was going herself to see Jacob Adler.

I felt ashamed to tell the truth, but to my own sister I would not lie. "Not yet. Tomorrow he'll come."

With her big, smart-old-lady eyes like Mama's she gave me a look that told me what she was going to say before she said it. "Don't buy without he's coming. A fine young man but. . . ." She shrugged like she didn't want to say more.

"You don't think he'll come?"

"I don't think yes, I don't think no. Wait."

"He'll come. Why say you're going to buy tickets if you're not going to?"

"A man can think he's going to buy tickets, but maybe on the way he changes his mind. Maybe he thinks tickets cost money. Maybe he thinks, Why spend money when the season is slow, the day was bad, I made no sale? I have it cheap living with my brother. Better I should not be in such a hurry. Who knows what a man thinks when he starts to think."

"You talk like he's proposing marriage."

On her face the same look was still there.

"What would a respectable man think when he has a wish to spend money on a girl?"

I had no answer for her, for I was thinking the same

thing. But maybe in America it was different. Maybe a man who did not care for a *shadchen* wanted to find out for himself with one girl and then another. Maybe Mr. Levine bought a lot of tickets. Maybe he would buy a hundred tickets before he was ready to make a proposal. Such an idea did not appeal to me in any way, and to think about it made me feel uneasy. One thing it showed was not to buy a hat in a hurry. But on the other hand, it hurt to believe he was not going to come with the tickets.

On Tuesday I wore my blouse with the blue embroidery again and sat with my face to the door.

"*Nu*, you're waiting for the Messiah to come?" Such a comment from Sam was not unusual, as he was the kind of man who had something to say about things that were not his business.

I paid no attention to him. What he thought did not concern me. For myself, I thought if Mr. Levine, a silk salesman, could make a fool of Rachel Ginsberg, better she should forget about tickets and about buying hats. Better she should think about the new line, about saving her own corset-cover money, about being independent and taking care of herself. But such thoughts did not stop me from looking at the door. What your mind says and what your heart feels are not always the same. In this particular circumstance, my mind was weak and my heart strong.

By Wednesday I said no more blouse with the blue embroidery. If Mr. Levine comes with tickets or if Mr. Levine doesn't come is ishkabibble with me. Still, it was foolish to move my worktable away from the door.

In the middle of the afternoon, when I looked up

from my sample, all of a sudden there was Mr. Levine.

"You're busy?" he said.

"Not so busy. Come in." Right away I thought, My hair, my old blouse. Why does he always come when I have given up?

"I don't want to disturb you." Such a gentleman. He should know that when he's not there I am more disturbed.

"Please, sit down."

"I can't stay," he said. "I just wanted to tell you I have the tickets for Saturday night. I hope that is convenient for you."

What I said, I don't know. He was standing right next to me, and our eyes were glued on each other. Like a piece of mush I felt, and I thought if he touched me I would faint. His bright blue eyes and pink cheeks, hair like red gold, lit up our shop like a bright light. He said, "I'll pick you up at six o'clock, and we can have a bite to eat before we go to the show."

Before I could breathe again he was gone.

He was in and out so fast I thought maybe I had imagined his visit. But Sam showed his head around the corner and asked who was there. I told him Mr. Levine, and he looked like he could see into my head. "Oh, so that's why you're all *fartootst*." He gave a loud laugh. "High-and-mighty Rachel's not so independent after all."

Such a comment I wouldn't dignify with a reply. To myself I thought that working all your life was not enough. When God put together the human body He gave it blood and feelings and a heart, and not to use such blessings would be a waste. Like the *shmattes* I

used to make the skirts, parts of me that had been lying
wasted were waking up and coming to life. For good or
for bad, Rachel Ginsberg was now a woman who was
going to get more from life than making dresses for the
line each season.

"For a silk salesman a shawl isn't good enough?"
Mama said.

"She has to have a hat," Inez told her. My little sister,
Inez. With my mind on other things, I had hardly paid
attention to her. At sixteen, she was already a grown-up
lady, *kayn aynhoreh*, with a figure and an air. She still
went to school, but also she worked. Never at the same
job for long. One time it was the bakery, the next a
shop that made wedding gowns. Maybe later she would
settle down. My hope was still that she would be a
teacher. But how to dress she knew; even in an old rag
she looked good. "I'll go with you to buy a hat," Inez
offered.

In the store she was fussy. "I'm not going to be in the
show," I said, "just looking at it." One hat was too big,
another too square, and another was a color that didn't
suit her. We both had to laugh when she put a hat on
my head that made me look like a coachman. At last the
saleslady brought the right one. A dark-red velvet Inez
said would be beautiful with a pair of earrings she
would lend me.

On the way home we walked arm in arm. "You like
this man very much?" Inez asked me.

"Who knows yet? But, yes, I like him."

"Rachel, don't let Mama tell you what to do. If you
like a man a lot, don't let anything stand in your way."

From my little sister I wasn't used to getting advice.

She gave me the feeling that she wasn't talking just for me, but for herself, too. "He has to like me too," I said.

Inez laughed. "How could a man help it? If a man likes you at all, he's going to like you a lot. For an ordinary man, you may not be right—a strong girl like you. But for the man who appreciates you, there will never be another woman."

Such words, like a wise old woman she spoke. There was a look on her face that didn't make me so happy, but I didn't want to bother her with questions. Maybe I was going to be sorry later, but I had the feeling whatever she had on her mind she wanted to keep to herself. As for me, I didn't want to be a buttinsky.

When Mama made her prayer over the *challa* on Friday night and lit the candles, I think that she prayed especially for me. Which way she was praying, who knows? In my bones I felt her prayer was not the same as mine and whichever God answered would not please one of us.

On Shabbes, I was already dressed early in the afternoon. With her lips Mama said nothing, but with her eyes she said a mouthful. Finally she couldn't keep still any longer. "You going out?"

"Mama, you know I'm going to see Jacob Adler. Don't make a game."

"Games? Who's making a game? I'm a mother. A mother doesn't make a game with her daughter."

"So, what's the matter? You don't like Mr. Levine?"

Iz was sitting in the room cleaning his nails. "She wouldn't like anyone for you. Except maybe the Prince of Wales," he said. "Don't you know, Rachel, with Mama you're a princess. Her favorite."

"I have no favorites," Mama said, but her face said

something different. Such an idea had never come to my mind. But all of a sudden I understood it was true. Iz was right. In Mama's eyes, no man would be good enough for me, except maybe a millionaire, and then he would need to have a college education and be perfect like a saint. Even so Mama would find fault. Such a thought made me feel uneasy. I didn't want to disappoint Mama. On the other hand, if no man was going to be good enough, a Mr. Levine or a Mr. Somebody Else would make no difference. So let it be Mr. Levine. As for being her favorite, Iz didn't use the right word. Mama gave out her love evenly to all three of us, but maybe, like Inez, she was worried that every Chaim Yankel would not care for me. She knew that I liked to be in business and maybe that I liked to be boss. What she didn't know was that a girl was different with her mama than with a certain man. That a Mr. Abe Levine with one look could make her forget the samples, forget the orders, forget the unpaid bills. There are times when a woman doesn't want to be strong. Sometimes she wants to lean on somebody else, share her worries with somebody else. Perhaps I couldn't lean on Mr. Levine as far as money was concerned, but I could with other things, more important things. I had plenty of experience myself handling money. For that, I didn't need a man.

At six by the clock Mr. Levine was at the door. He greeted Mama and Esther and Iz and Inez, and for little Nathan he had a bag of candy. But soon we left. On the street, he kept looking at me sideways. "You look very beautiful tonight," he said. "I'm proud to be with you."

"I'm glad you like my hat," I said foolishly. Such compliments I wasn't used to.

"It's not your hat, although it's very nice. It's what in it that counts."

We went uptown to Second Avenue where the theater was, but first we stopped to eat. It was a pleasure to watch Mr. Levine eat. He didn't pick at his food like Iz sometimes did, but he ate as if he was enjoying every bite. A man like that, I was thinking, would be a pleasure to cook for. He surprised me by asking, "A penny for your thoughts?"

His question struck me funny, and without a thought to what he would think I told him, "It's a pleasure to watch you enjoy your food. Your sister-in-law, I suppose, likes to cook for you."

"I like good food. Unfortunately, she is not a good cook. You like to cook?"

"I don't mind. At home Mama does most of the cooking. I work all day."

"Yes, of course. In your own home, though, would you like to cook?"

"I would never want to give up my business. In my home Mama would cook, too. She is a good cook."

"You mean she would live with you when you got married?" He was looking at me carefully. For me the conversation was getting a little finicky.

"Where else?"

"You have two sisters. Maybe she'd like to live with one of them."

"If she had to choose, I think Mama would want to live with me." Mr. Levine should know from the start how it was with me and Mama. He should know also

I was not the kind of person who would try to fool anyone. My heart did not like so much what I had to say, but there was no other way.

"But I think your mother doesn't like me." He spoke as if we had been talking about something else. Then he laughed. "You don't know me very well," he said, "but I should warn you right now that I intend to marry you."

His eyes were laughing at me. I thought I should be insulted for a man to say such a thing to me just like that. In a restaurant, yet. Like he might say he intended to buy a cigar. But instead, my heart was jumping, and like a shameless woman I wondered what it would be like to have his mouth with his beautiful red mustache brush my lips.

"And I usually get what I want," he said, not laughing anymore. "I'm impatient, but I'm not going to press you for an answer. Not yet. I understand you'd want to get to know me better, so I'll wait."

"That's very kind of you," I said, coming back to my senses. I smiled at him like I might to a foolish child. "But I'm not sure that I intend to get married. And if I do, it will not be with someone who makes up his mind, but to someone who feels with his heart." Where I got so clever I don't know, but instead of making him angry, my remark pleased him.

"You mean you want to marry for love? That's what I thought. Me, too. If I wanted otherwise, I could go to a *shadchen*, couldn't I?"

"But love doesn't come overnight, one, two, three. With me, it has to grow."

"I guess that's where we're different. I've known

from the first time I saw you. It only took a while to get up my courage to ask you out. I knew from the beginning you were the one. Your mother may think I have little to offer you. I make no apology. But I'm strong and hardworking, and you will have my love and devotion for all of your life."

His words were beautiful music to me, but I sat quietly eating my pudding, as if we were talking about the weather. "Don't we have to go to see the show?" I asked.

Mr. Levine smiled at me. I knew now what the look in his eyes meant. It was a look I would want to see every day for the rest of my life.

"Yes, I guess it's time to go," he said.

12

"So a regular Friday-night customer we've got," Mama said, when we were preparing the Sabbath meal a month or two later. Often I came home early on Friday afternoons to help.

"What's the matter with that? Iz came every Friday night for a year before he and Esther got married," I told her.

"That was different. With Iz we knew his intention. We knew they were going to get married. With Mr. Levine, who knows? He's got a good appetite, and he can eat here for ten years and not get married."

I had to laugh. "But you don't want him to marry me. So why worry?"

"A mother hasn't got a right to worry when a young man comes around every Friday night and who knows what's in his mind?"

"Maybe I know."

Mama went on peeling the potatoes, but in her eyes there was trouble. "He propose to you?"

"Maybe yes, maybe no. What's the difference? You don't want us to get married, do you?"

"Is it wrong for a mother to have hopes for a daughter? To want a man with an education, with a profession?"

"You don't know Mr. Levine. He reads everything. He can speak from the Talmud. He reads Tolstoy, Dostoevsky, all the great Russian writers he knows."

"So that helps him sell silk? Will it help him to pay the rent?"

"I've got a business."

"*Oy, oy,*" Mama was gasping, like she couldn't breathe. Right away I gave her a sip of water. "*Oy,* you're going to support a loafer. Better I should drop dead this minute than to live to see my daughter go to business to support a man. A disgrace for the whole family. A stab in the heart you give me with such talk."

"Don't get so excited, Mama. For a woman to support a family is no tragedy. I wouldn't be the only one. Mr. Levine is no loafer. He could come into the business. We could use a good salesman."

This idea upset her only more. "*You* would take *him* into the business? For a bride to take her husband into the business? Such a thing I never heard of."

"Iz came into the business, didn't he? Is there a difference for Mr. Levine?"

"Iz was there at the start. A different story altogether. And besides, with the right marriage, you could give up the business. Why should you go to work every day and come home tired? What kind of a life is that for a woman? And who will take care of the babies? Who will bake the challah? Who will shop for the food, clean the house? You've worked enough already, since you were a little girl. Now you should live like a lady, fix up a pretty home, have pleasure with your own family."

"Mama, you don't understand. The business *is* my pleasure. I don't like taking care of a house, I don't enjoy washing the dishes, making the beds. To boil an egg is a hardship for me. You know, I let the water boil away, I make the egg too soft, too hard. It never comes out right. In the house I'm no good. Maybe it's my misfortune. To design dresses I like, to see the orders come in, to see the finished dresses go out. For me this is excitement; this is my life."

"And Mr. Levine would take a wife who doesn't boil an egg?"

"Yes, yes. We've talked about it. He knows what a *shlemiel* I am in the house. I've told the truth to him. He says he doesn't mind. Mama, I think he loves me."

Mama sat so quietly I was afraid. When she spoke, her voice was sad. "You break my heart. I'm an old woman, and I know more from life than you. Love is fine when you're young, before the wrinkles come and the gray hair. But between a man and a woman, a man must be a man and a woman a woman. It's no good when you try to turn it upside down. A man must have his self-respect, must earn the money to take care of his family. The wife cannot do it for him. All your talk about excitement and pleasure is *bubkes*. It means nothing when you share a home, a bed with a man. You take the back seat and let him drive the horses. Otherwise, you mark my words, his love will disappear."

"Maybe in your day, Mama, but now things are different. Women want to get an education, too. They don't want to take the back seat. For me it's too late for an education, but I take the back seat to no one. A man who wants to do the driving alone should not be interested in Rachel Ginsberg. Already with my partners I've established a business. I've got a right to choose how I want to live. I ask favors from no one. If a man wants to marry me like I am, all right. If not, he should look for someone else."

Mama sighed, like already I was in trouble with my marriage. "Cheer up, Mama. I'm not married yet, so don't worry."

"Don't worry. . . . *Alevai*, I shouldn't worry."

Mr. Levine and I, we talked, but we never said too much. Without speaking, we understood. I was never much of a talker, but with Mr. Levine I could say what was in my mind and what I felt in my heart. Best of all, I liked to listen to him. What I said to Mama was the truth. He read all the time; like me he was never without a book. He could talk about them, tell me their stories, so it was like I'd read the book myself. It was a pleasure to listen to him, better than any show. He was like no other man, never coarse, with a respect for the things in life that mattered. When I walked down the street with him, he would stop to admire a special building or to say hello to a lonely child. In the park he would lie on the grass and look up at the sky and say things to me that were like poetry. He knew so many subjects. Better than the newspaper, he could explain to me about politics, about elections. Mr. Levine could tell me about Mr. Roosevelt and Mr. Taft, about the Democrats and the Republicans, who was right and who was wrong, and in his opinion why.

I was like someone under a spell. So busy with my own affairs, I had eyes for no one. Mr. Levine and I were going together for quite a long time, when one day Inez came to the business. She said she needed to have a talk with me. I looked at her for the first time in months, and with a pain I saw she was pale and tired. The expression on her face made her look older but also more beautiful, like a piece of silk that becomes more soft, more delicate after it's been worn.

Right away I knew she didn't want to talk in the place. So I put on my hat, and we went to a coffeehouse. She looked like she could use some food, but she said she wasn't hungry. We both had tea. No questions I asked. What was on her mind didn't come out in a hurry. First she asked me about me and Mr. Levine, and I told her the truth.

"A very nice man. A man you can talk to, a kind man. Maybe not a man who cares to make a lot of money. He has other things in his head. A disposition that is always interested in the world, what is going on—"

"Do you love him?" Inez asked. She leaned across the table, her big eyes looking at me.

"How do I know about love? To be with him is a great pleasure for me. I think I would like it for all the time, but how do I know?" To myself I was thinking, My baby sister knows more about such things than I. I knew so little of the world, thinking all the time about work, knowing only what I read in books.

"I think you're afraid to admit you're in love. You look like someone in love. I can tell. Remember what I told you. Don't let Mama change your mind. You have to do what you want, lead your own life." Inez's English was so much better than mine, and she talked with a great seriousness. But I didn't think she came to talk about me and Mr. Levine. I waited. There was plenty of tea to drink.

"I have something to tell you," she said, when I thought she would never get to what was on her mind. "Please don't scold me, don't be angry. I thought because you're in love yourself you would understand. I'm in love, very much, and I'm going to get married."

"Ida—Inez—my little sister. In love. A *mazel tov*! Why should I be angry? You think I care that you get married first when I am older? Maybe Mama will care for a little while, but she'll get over that. Who is the man? Why haven't you brought him to the house? Because of me?"

Inez gave a shake to her head. "That's not the reason." She stopped and drank her tea. "I'm almost afraid to tell you. Rachel, he's not Jewish."

A good thing my glass of tea was on the table, not in my hand. I would have dropped it. Such a shock. Yet something in me was not so surprised. I should have known. That made me feel worse about the news, as if somehow it was my fault. I had paid no attention to Inez. I had been so busy with my own affairs that I had not wondered who she was seeing, what she was doing. And who else was there? Esther had her husband and child to worry about, Mama went out of the house so little she could not know what was going on. I was the one responsible. My heart was sick.

"Maybe you just think you love him," I said. "Maybe it's something that will pass. You are still so young, only eighteen." Myself twenty-two, I felt years older.

"I've thought of all that. I've even tried not to see him for a while. But it's no good. I love him, and I'll never love anybody else. I can't live without him. He feels the same way about me. His family is Catholic, and they won't like it any more than mine. But we're going to get married. And Rachel, I want you to stand up with me for the ceremony. Will you?"

"Who will marry you? A Catholic and a Jew?"

"We'll have a civil marriage. In City Hall we can get married."

"Not by a rabbi?" Of course it couldn't be by a rabbi, but that was a bigger shock than anything.

"No, nor by a priest. But it's legal, just like a religious wedding. We love each other, Rachel. We can't help it."

"Tell me about him. What is his name? What does he do?"

Her eyes lit up like stars. "He's very handsome. Tall and dark. His family comes from Italy. He was just a baby, two years old, when they came here. Almost like a one hundred percent American. Dino, Dino Gallucci his name is. His mother and father run a restaurant on Mulberry Street, and he works there. Someday the restaurant will be his. He's hardworking, but like you say about Mr. Levine, he's lively, always with a smile. Sometimes in the restaurant he sings, and oh, such a beautiful voice, it could tear out your heart."

"But if he marries you, maybe his family won't want him in the restaurant anymore."

"He's the only son. The others are girls. He thinks his family will not throw him out. He says they'll get over being angry."

To think about it brought one terrible thought after another. "This will kill Mama. What about the babies? What will happen when they come along?"

Inez gave me a look and then turned her eyes down to the glass of tea in her hand. "If Dino wants to stay with his family, not to lose the restaurant, they will have to be Catholic. But what difference does it make?" she asked in a voice that was sharp, not like her own.

"What difference does it make what church you go to, if you believe in God and live a good life without harm to anyone? I will still be a Jew even if I'm not married by a rabbi. Nobody can change what you are inside."

"But your children will not be Jews. How can a Jewish mother have Catholic children? Sooner or later you'll be a Catholic, too."

"That's not true," Inez cried. "Dino says he will never ask me to change. Only the children, and that's for the sake of his parents. Not for him, he doesn't care."

A pain was growing between my eyes and on my chest. Like a bad case of indigestion, such a heaviness. "What about Mama? How are you going to tell Mama?"

She looked at me with eyes like a beggar's on the street. "I thought . . . I hoped. . . . Rachel, would you tell her? Please, I beg you. Can you do that for me? I'll never ask you for anything else in my life."

For a long time I couldn't answer. "Do you know what you're asking me to do? To take a knife to our mother's heart. No, it's not a thing you can ask another person to do. No. . . ."

"But don't you see? It will be better that way. Better for Mama. Maybe if you tell her, she won't think so terribly of me. She respects you more than anyone, and from you the blow would be softened. You can explain to her better than I that it is not such a crime, that love happens with a person, not a religion. Coming from you, it will be easier for her to forgive. Please, Rachel, I will do anything in the world for you if this one thing you can do for me."

"Anything in the world but one thing," I said, with a smile that wasn't a smile.

"No, don't ask me to give up Dino. That is impossible."

"I'll have to think about it," I told her. We sat and we talked. Inez said they wanted to get married maybe the next week. I asked why in such a hurry, and she said why to wait. "And where will you live?" I asked.

"In the beginning, over the restaurant with his family."

"You'll be happy to live with people who don't want you?"

"They like me. They don't know yet we will be married, but Dino says so long as the children are brought up Catholic they will forgive him. At first maybe it won't be so good, but the way they love Dino, they will not turn against him for long."

One thing I told Inez was that we shouldn't tell Mama until the day she was going to be married. My worry was that Mama would not let her in the house, and then where would she go? She agreed that would be best. To carry such a heavy secret was going to be a burden I did not care for. I could see why if Inez was going to do such a thing, it was better to get it over with than to live with a falseness between her and Mama.

13

I hope I never live through such a week again the rest of my life. Esther, who is no fool, knew something was going on, and Mama did, too. But my mouth was sealed like with glue.

I had to talk to someone, and thank God for Mr. Levine. By then he had asked that I call him by his first name, Abe, and if he could call me Rachel. I saw no reason why not, although for a while I could not get used to it. Mama, of course, made a face when she heard me speak of Abe, but I thought, poor Mama, that should be her only worry. A much bigger trouble she has coming up than Abe Levine.

Mr. Levine—Abe—was understanding like he was a brother. First he asked why should I do the dirty work. Inez should do the talking to Mama herself. I was too good, he said. We were sitting on a bench in the park on a beautiful day. I was thinking on a day like this, with a man you liked so much, it was too bad to have to talk about trouble. But that's the way life is; you cannot always pick the right day for the right talk.

But after we talked awhile he changed his mind. Abe was not a stubborn man who thought everything he said first was right. "Maybe it will be better for you to tell your mother," he said. "I'm an outsider, but I can see how it goes in your house." He smiled. "They look up to you."

"You think I'm bossy?"

"Not exactly. Not bossy like it says in the dictionary. You're too gentle for that. It's more that they depend on you. They respect you." Such a compliment from him was music to hear.

At last the day came for little Inez to get married. As she asked, I agreed to go with her. To be a bride all alone would be too much of a heartache for my baby sister. The day before, I persuaded her to go to the *mikva*. At least that much she should do out of respect for our religion. The day of the ceremony I left the shop before lunch and said I had some things to do. I went downtown to meet them in the park outside of City Hall. It was a cool but sunshiney day in May, and the park was pretty like a picture. From a little way off I could see the two of them walking arm in arm. I had to admit they were a beautiful couple. Like a princess Inez looked, tall and slim, wearing a pale-lavender dress with lace around the neck and a big hat. A beauty, not like a poor immigrant girl. And the man was handsome like someone on the stage—dark, wavy hair and a thick mustache. Also tall, with a fine figure. If only he was a Jew, I thought, Mama would be so proud.

When Inez introduced us, he put his arms around me and kissed me on the cheek "Thank you for coming with us. It means a lot to Inez and to me, too, my sister."

Already I was his sister. But I could tell he was speaking from his heart, not from being too forward, and right away I had to like him, Jew or no Jew.

"Did you tell Mama?" Inez asked.

"No, not yet. I'll tell her after I get home. After it is all done. Better that way."

"Will you come to the restaurant tonight? Dino wants to have a little party. Bring Mr. Levine with you if you like. Also, I'll want to know what Mama had to say." I could see Inez was nervous.

"What about Mr. Gallucci's parents? What did they say?"

"Please, not Mr. Gallucci. Call me Dino," he said. He gave a shrug of his shoulders. "Mama cried. Papa said Jews were fine people, but I should marry a Catholic. Who could help loving Inez, though?" He looked at her with eyes like Abe's for me. "They'll calm down. Mama said if only I could get married by the priest, but I told her that was impossible. She felt better when I told her the babies would be Catholic. It will be all right, don't worry."

About his parents I wasn't worrying so much, I thought. Mama was the one who was on my mind.

The wedding ceremony was a nothing. One, two, three, it was over. Mama spends more time buying a chicken. They call that a wedding? To join two animals I would give more respect.

But Inez and Dino didn't mind. They were happy like two doves. Dino asked could he come to the house and get Inez's clothes, but I said better not. After I told Mama I would bring them to Inez.

Dino took us to a restaurant, and he ordered wine, which I was not used to in the middle of the day. But on such an occasion I drank a glass. In my heart my feelings were upside down. To be happy for Inez or not, I didn't know. He seemed to be a fine man, but I saw trouble ahead. What can come of a marriage when one has to give up her religion, her family ties, the birthright of her children? When the first love dies down, maybe she will be sorry, and then it will be too late. Between the two, instead of such love, there can grow something that is not good.

Such thoughts, however, I kept to myself. Already it was too late to speak of such things. On this day, at least, there should be nothing but happiness.

But my heart was heavy when I left them. For me there was still the terrible task to tell Mama the news.

I walked slowly up our stairs, like I never wanted to get to the top. From outside the door I could hear Mama humming and little Nathan laughing, and to myself I thought, That house won't be so happy for long. Opening the door was like going to my own funeral.

"You're home early," Mama said. "What's the matter? You're not feeling all right?"

"I'm not sick," I told her. "I don't feel so great, but it's not my health."

"Something happen? What is it?"

I sat down. I was beginning to feel sick, in fact. "Mama, I need to talk to you."

"You want I should leave you alone?" Esther asked.

"No, you should hear it, too."

Mama sat down. Esther took Nathan on her lap. Like a committee they were looking at me.

"You look sick," Mama said. "Rachel, my *shayne* daughter, are you in trouble? *Oy, oy,* that no-good Mr. Levine. I'm going to faint, but tell me first. Are you in a family way?"

"Mama!" I was shocked. "Mama, how could you think such a thing? Mama, calm down. Oh my, you could think such a thing could happen between Mr. Levine and me. . . ."

"Could happen between a man and a woman," Mama

said. "I'm an old woman, but a little bit about life I know. Such things happen, even in the *shtetl*. And in this country, who knows?"

"Rest your mind. That is not the trouble," I told her.

"So, what is?" Esther asked. "Don't keep us on pins and needles."

"All right. But don't get excited. It's good news maybe, but more bad news. Inez got married. Today she got . . . ." They wouldn't let me finish. Both of them at once. Inez got married without them? Who did she marry? Am I making a joke? Is she ashamed of her family?

"It's none of that. She married a nice man. The bad news is he is not a Jew. He's a Catholic."

Mama did faint. Esther ran for the smelling salts. I brought a little glass of *shnaps*. When she came to, I thought she would go off again, so terrible she looked. But no, Mama got up and looked me square in the eyes. "Is what you say true? You saw it yourself? Ida and this—this man got married?"

"Yes, Mama, it's true."

Without another word, she got a cloth and put it over the mirror. She picked up the scissors and tore a rent in her dress. Mama sat down on a stool and started to wail. Her daughter Ida was dead.

There was no talking her out of it. Esther and I, later even Iz, pleaded with her to be sensible. But she turned deaf ears to us. Ida's name she wouldn't mention. For seven days, as when anyone dies in a Jewish family, Mama sat *shivah*. Iz she couldn't persuade to get a *minyan*, but still she carried on.

Only once in her craziness was she like our mama.

The same night that Inez got married and I was packing up her clothes in a bundle, Mama, with tears on her face, gave me a small package. Not a real package, something wrapped in a piece of paper. "Put this with your sister's things," she said.

I went that night to Dino's restaurant. Not with Abe, for who could reach him just like that in Paterson, New Jersey? I gave Inez her clothes and the package from Mama. When she opened it, both of us were surprised. Inside the paper was a gold pin, an ornament Mama had owned ever since we could remember. Inez had liked always that pin. "She still loves me," Inez said.

But when I told her Mama was sitting *shivah* for her, Inez wept. Mr. and Mrs. Gallucci and Dino's sisters all were pleasant enough, but I wasn't much in the mood for a party. I drank a little wine and made some conversation with them, but to myself I thought, My little sister is with strangers. Everything here will be different. In our house, too, I thought it will never be the same. Our stylish Inez no longer will show me how to fix my hair or make for us the blintzes that were her specialty. All of a sudden it came over me that she would be gone. Not just married, but gone. She would not be in and out of the house with her husband, later with her children. We would not have the pleasure of a Friday-night family dinner with her and her family.

Sad and angry I was that such a misfortune should come to us. I wondered was it right in God's eyes for one to be Jewish, another to be Catholic? Why not everybody the same? But then I thought it wasn't our fault that people were different. It was not the Jews who had driven others from their homeland; we were the ones who had been driven out. We were the ones whose villages had been burned by the Cossacks, whose people had suffered pogroms. Others had wanted to rid the world of Jews, driving them from one country to another. They were the ones who made us different.

Funny thoughts to be thinking, sitting with my sister and her new family. I wished in my heart I could feel that everything was going to be all right. But the truth was I could not feel at home with these people, no matter how refined, when I remembered how much the Jews had suffered from the Gentiles.

Soon I said good-night to Inez and Dino and the others. "You will come to see me, won't you?" Inez asked, holding me tightly. "And maybe you'll bring Esther and Nathan?"

"I'll come. If Esther will come, I'll bring her. Take care of yourself. Always I'll be thinking of you."

"Me, too," she said.

On my way home I thought of so many questions I didn't ask. Was she going to eat *trayf*? In a Catholic house how could she eat kosher? Better I didn't ask, better I shouldn't know. That night and every night afterward I asked that God bless her and forgive her her sin.

14

A Gypsy I'm not. I wasn't gifted to see into the future. Yet I wasn't so far wrong when I said that after Inez left our life would be different. Mama was never the same. Right away she started to fail. No life, no spirit was left in her. She didn't care about cooking or eating; she only sat and looked out the window. Not even sewing attracted her. One day I made a discovery; God knows for how long it was going on.

Mama was coughing, coughing, and when she took her handkerchief away from her mouth I saw blood all over it. She tried to hide it fast, but I was too quick. "Mama, you've got to see a doctor."

Mama shook her head. "What good is a doctor? I've got the sickness no one can cure. I don't want no doctor."

All of us tried to argue with her. But, stubborn like a mule, Mama wouldn't budge. She had the terrible disease, consumption. We knew, too, no doctor could cure it, but all the same it would have made us feel better for a doctor to see her.

It was hard on poor little Nathan. Such an affectionate child, always hugging Mama, climbing on her lap, wanting to kiss her. But now Esther was afraid that he could catch the sickness from Mama. All the time she was pulling him away from Mama, and what could the child understand? It could break your heart to hear him cry he wanted to love his *bobbe*.

150

What should have been a happy time for a young girl, keeping company with a fine man like Mr. Levine, was instead a life with a cloud over it. Still, every Friday night Abe came to our house, and with his own eyes he could see there was a sadness there. So one time in the summer, to cheer me up, he said we should go to Coney Island on the next Sunday. To leave Mama for a whole day for amusement was not exactly to my taste, but Esther said to go, she would be home. Besides, she said, Mr. Levine was entitled to some attention. So I agreed to go.

A beautiful day it was, sunshine bright like gold. We went out on the subway and the elevated train. On the boardwalk there was a breeze with a smell from the ocean that made Orchard Street seem a million miles away. It was beautiful.

A day I'll never forget. In the amusement park Abe persuaded me to go on some rides, enough to frighten the wits out of you. Up and down and whirling around so you didn't know your top from your bottom, your back from your front. I hung onto Abe so that when we stopped I was embarrassed, but he said that was the fun and why did I think he took me on such rides? To tell the truth, I too enjoyed being so close to him. Once in a boat we went through a dark tunnel, and without a word Abe gave me a kiss. My arms went around him, and again we kissed right on the mouth. A feeling came over me like I never had had before. Right away I came to my senses and took myself away from him as far as possible, but in such a small seat I could not go very far. Abe laughed his head off, like I was doing something funny. I scolded him but only in a joking way, because why should I deny that to kiss a man so dear to me was a beautiful pleasure.

That evening before we went home, sitting in a restaurant that served kosher food, Abe said we should plan to get married. He wasn't asking would I marry him, but talking like already I had agreed. *Chutzpa* he had.

"You never have proposed to me," I said. I felt somehow that if I never had a serious proposal of marriage I would be cheated of a memory that I would like to look back on later.

Abe smiled with a smile that was over his whole face. "All right, I propose to you. Rachel, my dearest, will you marry me?"

"Right away, I can't say yes. To appear too anxious will put your nose up in the air. I will think about it," I said.

"All right. I give you five minutes to think about it. For two years we've been going together, so by now you have had plenty of time to think. But you should know that if you don't say yes I will put a dagger into my heart."

"Fortunately, a dagger you don't have at the moment. A kosher knife you would make *trayf*. So I will take my time and answer you in maybe five, maybe ten minutes. I don't take orders." We were so intent looking at each other with our jokes and our seriousness, we let our soup get cold.

"Rachel, I love you," Abe said.

Such was my nature that to say the words *I love you* did not come easily. In my heart I felt the love, but to say the words out loud was for me an embarrassment.

Nothing I could explain. Perhaps later, when I was more at home in the company of a man, I would be able to tell him. Abe, I think, was disappointed, but he was kind and did not make a comment or push me. Maybe he understood. But soon I did say, "Yes, I will marry you," and across the table he took hold of my hand and pressed it to his lips.

Mama was dying. We did not speak of it, but in our hearts we all knew. There was no sense nagging her to go see a doctor anymore. It was too late. All we wanted was for her to be peaceful, but the coughing was terrible. All night from my bed on the sofa I could hear her hard breathing, and the cough, cough. Many times during the night I gave her warm milk and honey to ease her pain. Already she looked like an old woman, shriveled and tiny, although she was not yet fifty years. Between Esther and me there were many conversations. Would it be better for Mama or not, for Abe and me to get married while she was yet alive?

Such a question was not easy for us to decide. For myself, I was not in the mood for a wedding. But to make Mama happy, I would put on a good face. The problem, more than a wedding, would be the moving. We could not all live together in such a small apartment, and to move Mama now in her condition might be too much of a hardship.

Naturally, Abe wanted us to get married. For him the sooner, the better, he said. But under the circumstances, he left it for me to decide. Also, there was the question of Inez. To get married without my beloved sister was a hurt just to think of, but Mama would not even tolerate hearing her name. Once, when Mama was more cheerful, I mentioned I would like a wedding with all the family around me. Especially I mentioned Inez.

"Inez?" Mama said. "We have no Inez. Maybe you are thinking of Ida. She died a long time ago."

I had to turn away my face so Mama would not see my tears. Never again did I talk to her of Inez. Poor Inez. I went to see her as often as I could, and she seemed happy enough with her Dino. Knowing how it was with Mama, she begged that she should come to see her at least once before she died. "It is not possible," I told her. "It would be too much for her in her weak condition. For you, too, it would be painful, because she would not speak to you."

It is a terrible thing when a family is cut away one from the other. The love in the heart is still there, but there is no way for it to be let out. It lies like a heavy lump in the breast with no nourishment.

Again I was thinking that too much religion can be as bad, maybe worse, than too little. What was the crime Inez committed that she and Mama, and the rest of us, should suffer so much? Yet to watch Mama dying was to admire and respect religion, too. She was never afraid, never had a word of complaint. Her religion was a part of her, not just for the High Holidays. To accept what God arranged for her was in her very nature. Religion for her was not on the Sabbath alone. Every day she believed and trusted that what happened was right, and to have pain and to suffer was an expected part of life.

Not me. I did not think that way. I got angry to see people suffer. To see Mama in pain broke my heart. I could not believe that God wanted it that way. More, I believed He expected man to make changes, to make improvements. Why else would He give man a brain to think and hands to work and eyes to see? For me to follow the laws of the Jews was right, since that was the way our people would stay together, but what was God's will I was not so sure. What you got in this world you had to make for yourself, no one, not even God, would do it for you.

In the end our talking about what to do accomplished nothing. One night Mama called out to me, and quickly I went to her. In my arms she died. She was so small and frail that she seemed like a little child. Thank God, her suffering was over, but to myself I thought of the hardship of her life. To come to this country alone with her children, and every day of her life to work so hard, never with any rest. Yet always she got pleasure from little things—extra meat from the butcher; Friday night, when her family sat down together for the Sabbath meal; her grandson, Nathan. In her life she got pleasure from everyday affairs, from this, from that.

For myself, I wished often for her disposition, but I was not so blessed. I was not content to live my life in a tenement, to have to worry about money to buy enough food, to see only other women wear fine clothes. I was not afraid of work, it was my enjoyment, but to have the work add pleasure and comfort to my life was what I wanted.

The funeral for Mama was simple. Nothing fancy. Inez came with us, and wherever Mama was now, I thought, she would forgive Inez and rest in peace that her daughters were united.

It was hard for me to believe Mama was no longer

with us. I felt all my life I had been leaning against a strong pillar and all of a sudden it had been taken away. Esther said to me I should not feel that way because I was strong, but she did not know how much my strength came from Mama. Everything was different now. With Inez out of the house and Mama gone, nothing was the same.

With life you never know what will happen, and out of misfortune good sometimes comes. In this instance, it was with Esther that there was an improvement. She had always taken a back seat, not speaking up and saying what was on her mind. But soon I noticed she was more independent. Now Esther ran the house; she bought the food and did the cooking. From Iz she demanded more respect, and she asked more about the business and about the money. Esther was no fool. Soon it came to be that she showed a good head for figures. Esther was the one who said we were giving too much credit to some customers and taking too long to collect our money. With Nathan now spending time every day with the Hebrew teacher, Esther came to the shop and acquainted herself with the books.

A real family business we had, and it prospered. Maybe it was the munitions factories. Although making guns was not to my liking, people had money to spend. For our dresses we got good orders and fair prices.

"It's foolish for us to wait," Abe said. "We should get married."

With Mama gone, I didn't want to live with Esther and Iz. I felt I would be an extra wheel. Also, Esther was with child again, and I thought they should have a home of their own. So I agreed we could set a time to get married. Out of respect to Mama, I said we had to wait at least six months.

Anyway, first we had to find a place to live. Esther and I didn't want to live far apart, so together we went to look for apartments for our two families. For the children, Esther wanted to live where there was more space, trees, a place to play away from the street. So a big move we decided on, up to Washington Heights. It was beautiful. Quiet like in the country, lots of trees, and after we looked and looked, we found two apartments, one above the other, in a good house. From the bedroom window we could see the river. One on the sixth floor, one on the seventh, and an elevator with a man in a uniform to take you up and down. On a Sunday we could walk on Riverside Drive and get a breeze from the river. We felt like millionaires.

Even six months was not so long after Mama was in her grave, so a very quiet wedding Abe and I had. Just my family and his, in the *shul*. No music, no dancing. I felt sad without Mama there, but I was not afraid to be with Abe. About what went with a marriage in the intimate sense, I knew nothing. For me, to love and trust were enough. I never asked or knew if Abe had ever been with a woman before. It made no difference. What happened in the past was of no interest to me. From that day on it would be husband and wife, and that was enough.

15

From the beginning Sam wasn't happy to have Abe come into the business. "No Abe, no Rachel," I told him. We made an agreement then: Sam one share, Iz one share, and Abe and me two shares. What work Esther did on the books she should get paid the same as if she wasn't in the family. Sam even called a lawyer, who made a contract we signed, like our word wasn't good enough. But maybe it was just as well to have business in writing, God forbid anything should happen in the future.

To be without Mama was a hurt I would never get over, but to have a home of my own with Abe was a great pleasure. Such modern conveniences we had. Electricity instead of a gas jet. You just pulled a chain and you had light. Abe insisted we have a telephone, which I wasn't so crazy about. To speak into it made me nervous, and the bell made such a noise when it rang that it scared me out of my wits. Each time the machine rang I thought maybe there was a fire or someone was calling to tell us bad news.

Little by little we bought our furniture. First, a beautiful solid-mahogany bedroom set with a dressing table where I could sit and arrange my hair in front of a mirror. Abe loved to see me at the dressing table. Like an actress he said I looked. To me that was not such a compliment, but since it gave Abe pleasure I accepted it. A living-room set we bought, and a dining-room set, too.

We bought only when we had the money to buy the best. Cheap things neither one of us liked. They would not last, and good money would be wasted. "Cheap is cheap and good is good," was an expression Abe favored, and with that I had no argument.

One day a big box came to our house, a present from Abe. Inside was a victrola to play records of music. After that we sat many evenings and listened to fine music right in our own home. Beautiful songs sung by Caruso, violin playing, piano playing. Anything you cared to hear, you could play for yourself. I only wished Mama could have been alive to enjoy such gifts with us.

The main worry I had in those days was that there shouldn't be trouble between Sam and Abe in the business. Abe was not a salesman like Sam was accustomed to. He didn't make jokes, he didn't jolly people along, and in his dress he was neat but nothing flashy. In such things Abe was what you might call quiet, a man who thought business was business and what he wore was his own affair. Also, Sam didn't think much of what Abe talked about.

"We need an authority on Dostoevsky to sell children's dresses?" Sam demanded one day, when he listened to Abe in the showroom with a buyer. "A know-it-all about the Yiddish theater. A little joke, a little fooling around a buyer likes. For a college education they don't come here."

"You got an order, didn't you?" Abe said. "You do the cutting, I'll do the selling."

"This time you were lucky. But I've been in this business longer than you. I know a thing or two."

"Maybe you do, maybe you don't. You want a vaudeville actor for a salesman? When the business falls off, you can get one."

Not a word crossed my lips, but there were times I thought Abe would be wiser to keep his opinions to himself. To discuss politics with a buyer did not seem such a smart idea to me. To say if President Wilson was right or wrong, to say he should send soldiers to Mexico, to here, to there, was not the business of a dress salesman. But Abe was my husband, and what he picked to talk about was his affair. That he had a mind of his own I knew before I married him.

But the business was doing fine. Soon we moved from Sixteenth Street to a loft on Twenty-seventh Street, and in the season we had forty operators working. We all worked very hard. Before eight o'clock in the morning we were in the shop, and never before six in the afternoon did we leave. I am not a person who looks for praise, but, if I say so myself, the samples I made were beautiful. Buyers came to us from the big stores, from cities as far away as Chicago, St. Louis, Detroit. Never did they have a word to say against my dresses. Each season I made them a little different: something new, a different cut, a different trimming. About a lot of things I was ignorant, but somehow I knew how to think up new styles in children's dresses.

But with prosperity there also come headaches. For me it was not such a big trouble, but for Sam it was a problem. That was the union. They wanted to organize our factory. "How come you forget you were so big for the union in the old days?" I asked him.

"I was on the other side," he said, with no shame. "Now I'm a boss. I know more. I don't want no union to tell me what to do."

Iz and Abe argued with him until they were hoarse. Iz screamed, "Shame on you! You want to live off the workers' backs. I'm a boss, too, but I know what it's like. We both came to this country with nothing, and look what we've got. But you want more. You want a strike too? Would that suit you better? The girls on the machines, they got to eat too." From Iz I wouldn't expect such screaming, but when you get hit on the head fighting for the union, you don't forget so fast.

For myself, I wasn't sure. I couldn't forget Eileen, and in her memory alone I wanted good conditions for the workers. Also, I couldn't forget what it was like in the sweatshop. But our workers had it pretty good already. I was worried that if the union came in we would lose out to our competitors. They could undersell us, and that would be bad. It was more of a problem than I thought at first.

To be frank, I respected Abe's and Iz's opinion more than Sam's, but we had all worked too hard to have our business spoiled by the union. I tried to put off making a decision.

But when I heard that Mandelbaum and his sons signed with the union, I voted with Abe and Iz. Mandelbaum was almost put out of business before he signed. His operators walked out, his cutter, too, the whole shop. Sooner or later, I thought, we would have the same trouble. We would have to sign. So why make a fight about it? Better to get along right from the start so there wouldn't be friction. We had good workers, and if they walked out on us, it would do no one any good.

So it was three against one, and finally, giving a little here, taking a little there, we signed with the union. Once it was done, it made me happy. No matter what you say, to be making money when you know what it's like to be struggling is not so comfortable. To see those around you going through what you had to go through doesn't make you feel good when you go home to your new furniture, your house with an elevator, your victrola.

On Seventh Avenue not all the bosses agreed. Like Sam, a lot of them fought against the union. Sam said because I was a woman I was softhearted. Maybe so. But putting that to one side, I told him, "Better for business my way. You'll see. Sooner or later, the rest of them will have to sign with the union, and first they'll have plenty of strikes and trouble. They'll lose out." I don't like to say I told you so, but I was right.

Soon after we moved to our new apartments, Esther had her baby. A *shayne* girl named Miriam after our mother. Every month she asked me the same question, "*Nu?* Anything yet with you?"

"Why don't you ask Inez? She's been married longer."

Abe said I worked too hard; maybe that was why I wasn't with child. A *bobbe-myseh*, I told him. With so many people asking me every month—Abe, Esther, Inez —I told him it made me nervous, and maybe that was why nothing happened. Even Sam looked at me with a question.

I was surprised Inez had no child yet. I didn't see her as much as I would have liked. Every night they worked in the restaurant, and in the daytime Abe and I worked. Sometimes, when we were not too tired, we went to Mulberry Street to visit, but we couldn't eat in a non-kosher place. What I saw in the restaurant I didn't like so much. Very neat and clean they kept it, but I could see that there wasn't much money to spend. Things looked poor. Some paint wouldn't have hurt, maybe some new seats on the chairs, and Inez, who enjoyed clothes so much, never had something new to wear. Always when I left there, I had a pain in my heart. For Esther and me to have more was fine, but that our baby sister, Inez, should always be worried about the bills was a heartache.

It was no surprise to me when one day Inez came to the factory and asked me to come out someplace to talk. Right away I knew there was trouble. I remembered how she came the same way to tell me she was getting married. You never know what life brings, I thought. So much I had hoped for little Inez. She could have been a teacher, and now she was spending her time, day and night, in an Italian kitchen, not even kosher.

We went to the dairy restaurant and sat at a table. "How is everything?" I asked her.

"So-so. I'm going to have a baby." She looked at me with her big eyes, but I could see she wasn't altogether happy.

"*Mazel tov.*" I leaned over and kissed her. "Good news."

"Not all so good. Why beat around the bush? Rachel, we need money. Do you think maybe you could lend us a few hundred dollars?"

To give her the money I didn't care, but to see her look so worried I didn't like. "How much exactly do you need?"

She was pale like a ghost. "Do you think you could manage five hundred? We'd pay it back. I can't say exactly when, but we can pay interest the same as you'd get from the bank."

"Interest from my own sister? You must be *meshugge*. I'll manage. You need it right away?"

"As soon as possible."

Not much conversation we had. I didn't want to ask questions, for I could see she had plenty of *tsuris*. "Dino is a good man," she said. "He works hard. But everything is so expensive. It's hard to keep up with the bills. If our credit is cut off, we'll be out of business."

"Yes, I know." I thought to myself, Maybe better to be out of business than to keep on losing money. Yet I didn't want to butt into her affairs. Before we parted we arranged to meet at the bank the next day. I had saved a little money of my own, so I could give it to her without having to go to the business. Better not to mix up Sam and Iz in a private affair.

"Don't worry about giving it back. When you have it, all right; if you don't have it, that won't be so terrible either."

"What would I do without you, Rachel?" Inez said.

"You'd live."

I was happy for Inez to be getting big with her child, but why not me? I wondered. Was God punishing me for not staying home like a good Jewish wife? Was Abe right, that because I was working, I was not getting with child? I am ashamed to admit that I was jealous of my sisters. Esther with her Nathan, already a big boy, and her little Miriam, God bless them. And now Inez, with all her troubles, looking more beautiful than ever in the family way.

In due time her baby arrived, a beautiful boy she called Richard. Who knows where she got the name, but she was so happy I asked no questions. To hold him in my arms was a sweetness that made me happy and sad at the same time.

Maybe I should forget about having a child, I thought. To worry about it so much could be the trouble, so I tried to put it out of my mind. I had my niece and nephews to enjoy.

Then, when I least expected it, it happened. That's the way life is. Almost four years we were married when I could tell Abe the good news.

Like a *meshuggener*, he wanted to buy cribs, baby carriages, blankets, booties. "Nothing we buy until the time comes. Pick them out maybe, but nothing in the house before," I told him. To Abe I wouldn't say it, but I thought it would be bad luck, God forbid, to have everything ready ahead of time. Every few minutes he asked how was I feeling, did I want a cup of tea, I shouldn't be on my feet, maybe I wanted to lie down.

Never an angry word we said to each other, but for nine months to have such craziness, I thought, was too much. "I'm a healthy, strong woman," I said to Abe. "To have a child is not a sickness. If you carry on this way, maybe I will get sick." That quieted my Abe down, but even so he treated me like I was a china doll.

Esther was almost as excited as he was. "You'll stay home when the baby comes, and we'll take our children out together. It will be nice, Rachel. The way Mama would like it, may she rest in peace."

To discuss the future right then I didn't think was smart, but I had no intention of staying home like

Esther, even though I knew, too, Mama would like it. For Esther it was fine. With her Nathan and little Miriam, she was blooming like a rose. Already she knew everybody in the neighborhood, and always in her kitchen you could find a coffee klatch. Also, she joined Hadassah, a new organization of women to help with health conditions in Palestine, fine ladies who respected Esther. There she was a real *macher*. But for me it would not be a life. Maybe when God made me, He left something out. To be Abe's wife, and to look forward to being a mother, made me very happy, but to make that my whole life didn't satisfy me. Sometimes it came to my mind that I wanted too much, and maybe that was a sin. To want something for herself was perhaps wrong for a woman. Why shouldn't I be content to stay home like Esther, to take care of the children, to buy the food and cook the supper? To talk with the other women about the children and the house?

But I had to be honest with myself. Wrong or right, my interest was in the shop. Even if I stayed home for a day because I was not feeling well, my head was there. Did the buyer from J. C. Penney come in? Did Sam get out the order to ship to St. Louis? The lace I ordered, did it come in? Everything went through my mind. To stay home was a bigger hardship than to go downtown, even if I wasn't feeling a hundred percent perfect.

Every day I went to work, until the seventh month, when Abe said I must stay home. *Oy*, those two last months. They lasted a long time. I was not so big, but I felt like a mountain. Esther had been knitting and crocheting, so I had a few things. Also, I made some infant dresses—so beautiful, all done by hand, not a stitch on the machine.

When my time came, the pains started around midnight. Abe got Esther to stay with me, and he went for the midwife. His idea was for me to go to the hospital, but I refused. I saw enough hospital the time I had to find Iz. You can have the hospital, I told him, not for me and my baby.

I did not have an easy time. All night, all the next day I had pains, but the baby did not come. Even the midwife, a jolly woman, was getting nervous. I had to tell her to calm down. At last, three o'clock in the morning, the baby came. A beautiful little girl. So little, not even the size of a good roasting chicken, but everything perfect, ten little toes, ten little fingers. A miracle.

A blessing we had with our baby. I had decided on the name long before. Maybe Abe didn't like it so much, but he was so happy that he'd agree to anything. If Esther didn't have her Miriam, naturally I would have called her after Mama. But with a Miriam already in the family, I could indulge my fancy and give in to a sentiment from long ago. Eileen I called her. "An Irish name," Esther said, not so pleased.

"Maybe Irish, maybe not. Who knows? A pretty name, and after my friend. I always liked that name, and such a fine girl for my daughter to be called after."

Now we all had children. Four one hundred percent American children, God bless them. May they all grow up to be healthy and happy and prosperous.

16

With happiness the days go fast. It seemed in no time little Ellie (Abe gave her that name as Eileen was too fancy for him) was too big for her crib and we had to buy a bed. Already she was trying to walk, and she was saying "Mama" and "Papa" like she was born with a golden tongue. Such a smart child I never saw, and beautiful like a picture, if I must say so myself. A blessing she was every day of our life.

In the beginning, we had trouble finding a good, honest girl to take care of her. Blacks, Irish, German, one after another we had, but one took the *shnaps*, one was so dirty, you could die from the smell, another was making with the cross over her all the time, saying prayers, who knows what? At last, we got Julia. Not the smartest girl in the world, but honest, good-natured, and Ellie took to her like she was in the family. A plain cook, nothing fancy, but also the food was not greasy. She had every Thursday afternoon and every other Sunday off, and the silver I didn't have to count. I could go to business with an easy heart. Now for the telephone I was thankful; should anything happen, Julia knew how to call me.

But in the business everything wasn't always smooth. Like I said, if Sam had a chance, he would find something to criticize in my Abe. Once in a while he had a reason. Abe belonged to his Minsk society, and naturally his *landsleit*, when they could, came to give him business. It so happened that one Mr. Greenberg owned a small department store in Newark, New Jersey, and he gave Abe an order for dresses. A new customer, but a *landsman*, Abe gave him credit. To make a long story short, Mr. Greenberg got the dresses, but we never got his money. Sam's screaming you could hear all the way from Twenty-seventh Street to Washington Heights. You'd think a million dollars Mr. Greenberg owed.

I can't say Abe was a hundred percent correct, but to do a favor for a friend is no crime. Although I have to admit that when it comes to business, you've got to treat friends like everyone else. What made the most trouble is that Sam right away wanted his Saul (already working for a law office) to sue for the money. That little snot nose, Saul—I wouldn't give him a case if I was dying.

Already things had been a little cool between Lena and me. She made remarks I didn't care for. Maybe Sam should get a bigger share of the business, she said. So I told her maybe he would like to sell his share. I could get another cutter without much trouble. If he wasn't satisfied, he should take his money and go. But I noticed she had a new fur coat and a diamond pin. I didn't begrudge her, she should enjoy. She too had had it hard, and to have Sam for a husband was no picnic. But I didn't think she had a right to complain. I don't like to put credit on myself, but if left alone Sam would still have been a cutter in someone else's factory. Instead of geting laid off in the slack season, he was a partner in one of the best houses on Seventh Avenue.

Abe and me, we too liked a little enjoyment out of life. Fur coats I didn't care about. Nice things for the house I liked, and Esther and I bought beautiful silver candlesticks and cut glass fit for a palace. My greatest pleasure was when the four of us went to the opera. Abe and Iz bought us diamond pins and necklaces, and Friday afternoon, before I came home, I met Esther at the bank, and we took our jewelry from the box in the vault. Together, we often laughed until we cried. The two of us, like grand ladies, getting our jewels to dress up on Saturday night for the opera.

"Two Kuni Lemmels," I would say. "If Mama could only see us."

"Only in America," Esther said. "Only in America could two immigrant girls have such finery."

"Could have a business," I said. For me, I could never get over the miracle of the business. Sometimes in the night I'd wake up and think, Will it be there the next day? Maybe I'm imagining the business, and tomorrow it will be gone. But the business was there, and, knock wood, it was doing all right. To be millionaires I didn't care about. To support three families was enough, and each year it was improving.

Ellie was a year old, maybe a little more, when everyone was frightened by an epidemic of influenza. I told Julia to keep her away from other children, and around her neck I tied a square of camphor to keep away the germs. But such a worry, I can't tell you.

"We should take her out of the city," I said to Abe. "In the country there will be less danger."

Abe agreed. We talked it over with Esther and Iz, who were worried the same way about their Nathan and Miriam, and we decided to take a house together on Long Island by the ocean. So one Sunday, a beautiful day in June, the four of us took a train to Far Rock-away. It was beautiful. Just the smell from the ocean was enough to make me know this was the right place.

A man from a real-estate office showed us houses, and the second one he showed us, Esther and I knew right away it was the one for us. A house I had only in my dreams. A big house with a wide porch all along the front and the side, a large living room, a dining room, a room the man called a "breakfast room" ("You can't eat lunch there?" I asked), a kitchen, and a pantry. Upstairs a bedroom for the two girls, another room for Nathan, one for Esther and Iz, one for Abe and me, and two bathrooms. And a third floor besides, with a big attic and two rooms and a bath for the cook and the nursemaid.

Sam's whole apartment that we lived in when we first came to this country you could put into one room. Still, the best part for me was that I could sit and watch the ocean from the porch. Already the house had furniture in it, and what more we needed we would buy. We agreed to rent it for the summer, and if we liked it, we could buy it in the fall.

Outside, Esther and I stood and looked at the house like we couldn't believe it was real. In front, a beautiful green lawn and two rows of rosebushes along the path from the street. Also, in back, apple trees and pear trees and plenty of space for a vegetable garden.

On the way home in the train Abe said we would have to buy a car. "It will be easier for you," he said to me, "than to take the train every day to work." Always Abe was worrying about my health. Sometimes I had a pretty bad cough, but so what? A cough is not so terrible, and the pain in my chest I didn't have to tell him about. Sooner or later it went away, and I'd forget about it until the next time.

Esther did most of the buying for the country house as I was busy with the winter line. She knew more about such things than I did anyway and enjoyed looking for bargains. When I needed something, I would go to an established store like B. Altman's or Wanamaker's, but Esther would go down to Orchard Street and dig out a bargain she could show off with pride.

In the business, my good friend was Clara, our Italian forelady, a hard-working widow. When she heard about our house on the beach and buying a car, she said, "Soon you won't want to come to work anymore. Such a fine lady."

"You know me better," I said to her. "With me work is my pleasure. Besides, all these things cost money and have to be paid for."

Clara and also Mr. Feinson, a salesman who traveled with our dresses together with some other lines, knew better than anyone that without my samples we'd have no business. Clara alone I could trust to make the samples exactly how I wanted them, not to take any shortcuts or skimp with the lace or the trimmings. And how the samples were, so were the orders. No different. To order from a sample and then get different dresses, I didn't like. Ask anyone on Seventh Avenue, they could tell you that our house was honest, our word was good as gold. What you ordered from us, you got exactly. Nothing was cheap about our dresses. Fine material, good workmanship, simple styles. Children outgrew our dresses; they didn't wear them out. Younger children in the same family could wear them long after they were bought.

Much as I enjoyed the business, when we moved out

to Far Rockaway for the summer, I cannot tell you how much pleasure I got from that house. To sit on the porch in the evening and smell the ocean, to hear the sound of the waves, it was like a dream come true. In the city with all the noise and hushy-bushy, it was easy to forget how sweet the air can smell, how beautiful the sounds of nature are. The car, too, was a great comfort. Abe and Iz bought a big, open touring car, and we hired a chauffeur, Roger. Every day except Saturday and Sunday he drove us into the city and took us back. For Esther and the children they bought a little Ford, which she learned to drive, God knows how. She did the shopping and took the children wherever they wanted to go.

You get accustomed quickly to such comforts, as if you had had them all your life. Often Esther and I talked about the children—Inez's Richard, too, who came and spent most of the summer with us. (Inez and Dino came only once in a while, except for one week when they closed the restaurant.) "Our children are growing up with everything given to them, no hardships," I said to Esther. We were sitting under an umbrella on the beach watching them play in the water. Nathan, already a grown boy, was out with his friends.

"Isn't that what we want for them?" Esther asked. "What we worked for?"

"Yes, but I'm not so sure. What if something should happen? Will they be able to take care of themselves?"

"Nothing's going to happen," Esther said. "If they have a good education, they will manage. The boys will have a profession and the girls husbands. Don't worry about them."

"All right. You say so, I won't worry."

To worry was not my specialty, but sometimes I did think how remarkable it was to see so much change in one lifetime. From Sam's apartment with the toilet outside in back, working on the knee pants (many times we had a laugh over the spilled pot of tea), to this house on the beach with a telephone and victrola, electric lights and two cars, and a cook and nursemaid and chauffeur. And our apartment in New York, now with the furniture covered with sheets and mothballs on the rugs. It hadn't been easy to get—years of hard work it had taken —but now the desire to hold on to it for the children was so strong that I had to wonder if it was good to have so much. Would our children be spoiled, not knowing any hardships? Would they expect life always to be easy, to have everything handed to them on a silver platter?

When I mentioned my thoughts to Abe, he answered, "Only good health is important. To lose money, the other things, is a hardship but not everything. Health is what's important."

At the end of the summer, I would have bought the house no matter what they asked. But we got a fair deal, and so now we owned a house in the country to spend our summers in. Like the rich German Jews.

17

Like Abe said, the important thing was good health. In those years our biggest worry was Ellie. So many diseases a child can get, and all of them came to Ellie. Measles, chicken pox, mumps, ear abscesses—every week it seemed it was something else. We worried about typhoid fever, rheumatic fever. Who knows all the things a little girl can get? We kept her out of school. We took her to Far Rockaway early in May and stayed until October. The fresh air and the ocean seemed good for her. A happy, active child, she broke our hearts when we saw her in bed, pale, feverish, and without an appetite.

I had my troubles, too. After those years of waiting, twice I was with child, and both times I lost the baby. The doctor said no more babies, and so that was that.

But the cough I couldn't hide anymore. One night Abe insisted we go to a movie house to see Charlie Chaplin. I never was much for the movies, but Abe enjoyed a good comedy, so I agreed. In the theater, however, there were men smoking (maybe women too, who knows?) and I got to coughing and couldn't stop. Abe took me outside, and he saw I was spitting up blood.

Oy, the way he carried on. You'd think I was dead already.

"It's nothing," I said. "I'm strong, healthy like an ox. Maybe from the beets I ate at lunch."

"You don't have food in your lungs," Abe said. "Tomorrow you go see the doctor."

What good could a doctor do? For what I had, the same like my mother, he had no medicine. I knew already before I went what he would say. Rest, stop working, take it easy. But Mama wasn't working, and still it got her. What was going to be, was going to be. If I had to stay home and rest, I might as well be dead. Who was going to get the line out? Who would show Clara how to make the samples? What would we have to show the buyers? And without new samples, where would the money come from for the rent, for the house in Far Rockaway, for the butcher, the nursemaid, the cook?

And the fine things I wanted for our Ellie. Already she was going to dancing school, taking piano lessons, going horseback riding in the summer. Every advantage in America our Ellie had. She was like a little princess, the daughter of immigrant parents who came to this country with nothing. Where else could such a thing happen? For this I would spit up a quart of blood, I didn't care. For everything you have to pay in this world. Nothing comes free. So now with all the fine pleasures we were enjoying from the years of hard sweatshop work, we also had to have a worry. To me it was no surprise. By this time I knew enough about life to accept that with the good always there had to be some bad.

The doctor said I should go to Saratoga Springs and take the hot baths. I didn't think so highly of his advice, but I didn't mind. If hot baths would cure me, I was willing. But something else he told me put fear in my heart as if he cut me with a knife. "Tuberculosis," he said, "you can give to your family. You must be very careful with your husband and your child." I should have remembered how Esther used to have to keep

Nathan away from Mama. But some things your head wants to forget.

What could be a greater hurt for a loving wife than to have to hold back affection from her husband? What pain can equal the pain of a mother who has to tell her child not to climb on her lap, who has to turn her face away from her daughter's kisses? I'm telling you, with that worry hanging over my head I wondered often if it was worthwhile to live. At least with Abe, as much as it hurt, he could understand. Without asking questions, I got rid of our big, four-poster double bed and bought a set of twin beds. Abe said our bedroom looked like a dormitory in school.

But with Ellie there was nothing to explain. She didn't know why she couldn't hug and kiss me anymore —such an affectionate child. It was heartbreaking when Julia had to pull her away from me. I had to hide my face so she shouldn't see my tears. Sometimes she got so angry that her little face turned red and she stamped her foot and screamed, "I hate her, I hate her. She doesn't love me anymore."

My heart hurt when Julia tried to quiet her down, and I tried to tell her how much I did love her, but she wouldn't listen. She put her hands over her ears and kept on screaming. I couldn't scold her. Already she showed signs of the woman she would be, a woman, like me, with passion, who needed to show her love and to accept love with more than words.

Such a situation between a mother and daughter and a wife and husband was terrible beyond words. Sometimes I thought maybe I should live my life out in a sanitarium with others like myself. But to go away from them completely I could not do, and also, without my samples, the business would not last long.

In June we went to Saratoga for a few weeks. It was nice. We stayed in a fine hotel, but I don't know what good it did me. Nothing changed.

The only change was that we moved again. Abe thought I shouldn't travel so far, so we moved downtown into an elegant apartment in the seventies. Esther and Iz also moved near us.

All the time I tried to hide from Abe my sickness, but I knew in my heart I did not have too long to live. To die I was not afraid. My beloved mother, my dear father, my friend Eileen, the two little babies I lost—all had gone before me. So whatever was in store for me would be the same as for them, and to have rest and peace and no more worry was not such a bad thing.

I was worried more about those who would remain alive. What would happen to my Abe and my Ellie?

Sam, I knew, had made out a will with his Saul. But I did not want to have any business to do with Saul. By now Esther's Nathan was a young man working in a law office. A smart young man going with a rich girl, Sadie Hertzberg. Soon we expected a wedding. It so happened that the owner of the law firm where Nathan worked was Sadie's father, and after the wedding Nathan no doubt would be a junior partner. Not that he didn't love Sadie—a pretty, educated girl—but for her father to be rich and the boss didn't hurt.

One day I called up Nathan and said I would like to see him, but I didn't want Abe to know. What was the use of worrying Abe more by telling him that I had made out my will?

I went to see Nathan in his law office, and I told him what was on my mind.

"It's a good idea to have a will, Aunt Rachel," he said to me. "You always were a smart businesswoman."

It was a relief he didn't ask questions. Let him think I wanted a will only because I was smart.

There was nothing that made a problem. I wanted to leave everything in trust to Ellie, except for some money and a few trinkets to Julia and several personal items to my dear sisters. The executors should be Abe and Nathan. Only on one point I had to argue with my nephew. When I died, and I knew but he didn't that the time wouldn't be far away, I wanted Abe to get out of the business. Maybe within a year.

"What's the point of that?" Nathan asked. "Such a prosperous business. But I suppose if you did go first, and I hope not, he'd be an old man by that time anyway."

"Old man or not, my Abe is not such a great business-man. And, if you'll excuse my saying so, neither is your father. I don't want to take credit on myself, but with-out my designs there'd be no business. To get a good designer, if they were lucky enough, would change the business, and before they knew it, they'd be out anyway. Take my word for it. Iz I can't tell what to do, but when I go, much better Abe should take his money from the business and invest it in good, safe United States Trea-sury bonds. Good as gold. Believe me better than to run a business."

That's the way I wanted the will to be, and that's the way he made it.

A few days later, when he sent me a copy and I signed it and put it in the safe-deposit box, I felt a great relief.

Whatever happened would happen, but I felt my loved ones were taken care of, and I could rest easy.

That summer, maybe because I felt another winter I wouldn't get through, was especially beautiful. We celebrated Ellie's tenth birthday with a beautiful party on the beach. Fifteen children we had. In the afternoon they went for a ride in a pony cart we hired. Such a good time they had. Esther and I had to laugh because for them a pony cart was such a treat when to us the automobile was still a miracle.

At the beach they all went bathing. Then Abe made a big fire there, and Julia and the cook brought out cold chicken and potato salad for the children. They roasted marshmallows on the fire, and we had a big birthday cake. Such a beautiful time. My only sadness was I couldn't take my Ellie in my arms and kiss her like my body was aching to do.

Every day that summer was precious to me. The cough was getting worse. I could see in Abe's face, in Esther's too, that I couldn't hide the truth from them any longer. We all knew it was going to be only a matter of months, maybe weeks, before I would leave them.

But I was stubborn. I wouldn't give in. And even Abe stopped asking me to stay home. He knew, too, it would make no difference. Finally I did stay home, in my bed where I could hear Ellie after school with her friends, laughing and playing, God bless them. I felt sad that I wouldn't see her grow up, wouldn't see her as a bride with her husband, wouldn't hold a grandchild in my arms. But I felt at peace, too. I had accomplished something in my life, and maybe my Ellie with her fine education, all the many things she was learning, all her advantages, would become someone really important. I was sorry to die, but not unhappy.

Abe was my great comfort. He didn't go around singing, but he kept a cheerful face most of the time. He spoke to me like when he first took me out. "You're beautiful, Rachel. I'm proud to be with you."

But it was to little Ellie my thoughts kept coming back. So much I could teach her if I lived. Still, she was smart. She'd learn by herself. After all, everybody had to learn for herself. "She will be a good daughter to you," I said to Abe. "You won't be lonesome. A fine American young lady she'll be. But don't let her forget where she came from. . . ."

Her life will be so different from mine, I thought, as I lay in my bed. I wanted it to be easier; yet I wished too that our struggle, Mama's and my sisters', Abe's and mine, should not be forgotten in all the advantages in America. All very well to enjoy comfort, but to put it first in your life was to ignore your religion, was to ignore the hardships of the Jewish people, was to forget what has made them strong. And every day one should remember how beautiful is the gift of life. If I taught my young daughter only that much, I could die content. . . .

Epilogue

Ellie didn't eat much of the supper she cooked for her father and herself that night. Her mind was on the document she had read that day and on her mother's will. She could almost feel her mother's presence, hear her voice asking, "What are you living this way for when I worked so hard for you to be comfortable?"

Ellie could hardly wait to go to the bank the next day to get the will from the safe-deposit box and read it for herself.

It was all there. All the provisions her father had told her about, the bequests no one had received. Ellie wept when she read the will, sad for her father and herself, terribly sad for her mother. And suddenly she felt a longing for her mother, a feeling that she had been cheated out of ever really knowing this remarkable woman who had done so much but had kept so much contained within herself.

"What are you going to do?" her father asked her.

"I don't know. I have to think about it."

To try to understand her mother, to understand her mother's will, Ellie decided to talk to everyone in the family: her aunt Inez, Uncle Iz, Cousin Sam and his wife, Lena. She would even go to their son, Saul, whom she knew her mother had disliked.

A week later she was still asking questions, trying to fit the pieces together, to understand.

"Why didn't they tell me that my mother had TB?" Ellie was sitting in her aunt Esther's comfortable living room. She still thought of it as Aunt Esther's house, although now Aunt Esther was gone, and her uncle Iz lived there with her cousin Miriam.

Uncle Iz's pale eyes examined her as if perhaps he had not really seen her before. "Your mother didn't talk about such things. No one did. It wasn't like today, when people don't care what they say."

"But that's nothing to be ashamed of. To be sick." Ellie was indignant.

"Ach, you understand nothing. About the body you didn't talk. Such private things you kept to yourself. Especially a woman like your mother. A woman ahead of her time, but a woman who didn't talk about her health. About the business she talked. We didn't always get along, but I always had respect for her. To herself she wouldn't admit she was sick, and to advertise it, never. You can hear all the stories about her from now until doomsday, but you won't understand. Never."

Uncle Iz was right. She had heard many stories about many incidents, and yet basically her mother was still a mystery to her. Her own memory was like a shadow that came and went. She knew there was a time when her mother laughed and was gay, hugged her and played with her. But then a curtain fell, and her memory was of someone remote, an austere woman, a woman she could not reach. A woman who went to business and came home from business, often had to lie down until dinner was served. Ellie remembered her own tantrums and the awful mixture of love and hate she had felt as, screaming, she had been stopped from hugging her mother.

Why hadn't they told her? Had her mother believed that she was indestructible, had she not been able to face her own mortality?

When Ellie left her uncle's apartment, she was headed for the last person on her list. The last and perhaps most important of all, her cousin Sadie, Cousin Nathan's widow. Sadie had been in Florida visiting her own parents, and, so the family had told Ellie, to recover from the tragedy of her husband's death. Cousin Lena had admonished Ellie, "You shouldn't bother her now. It isn't right. It's no time to talk about money."

"Her lawyer didn't waste any time getting to me with the release," Ellie had shot back. "He wouldn't have known where to find me without Sadie telling him, so she must know. If they can talk about money, so can I."

Ellie had waited a few days after Sadie's return, but now she was on her way. Admittedly, she was nervous. She didn't know her cousin-by-marriage well, and the little she did know had not been endearing. She was what her mother would have called a "Miss Nose-in-the-Air." Stuck-up.

She had been to the Park Avenue apartment only once or twice, and now when she entered the marble-walled lobby she could feel her anger quickening. The bowing subservience of the Negro doorman and the elevator man when she told them whom she was visiting irritated her. Cousin Sadie must tip them lavishly she thought. The contrast between this show of wealth and her own dingy hotel was infuriating. She wanted to shout at someone, "Don't you know there's a depression? Don't you know that people are starving? Don't you know that my father and I, who once lived this way, now have nothing?"

Her anger was not only for herself and her father. Her anger was for the sad-eyed people who sat in her hotel lobby, for the men and women on the breadlines, the families living in the makeshift shacks. There was something indecent about this opulence when there was so much tragic poverty nearby.

Ellie was still angry as she sat in her cousin Sadie's elegantly furnished living room waiting for her to appear. She kept going over in her mind what she intended to say and hoped that neither her nervousness nor her anger would show. Keep calm, she told herself. In spite of her assurances to herself that she had been wronged by Cousin Nathan, she felt uncomfortable, as if she were asking for a favor, a handout. She didn't like the feeling.

She was lost in her thoughts when Cousin Sadie came into the room. Ellie was startled by how frail she looked. Her usually made-up face was pale, devoid of powder. She was dressed in black, and her hair was pulled away from her pretty face in an unbecoming knot.

Sadie walked right over to Ellie and took her in her arms. "You're so dear to come to see me," she said, and broke into sobs. "I want to stay close to Nathan's family. He loved all of you so much. . . ." She spoke between sobs until, with Ellie holding her, she finally quieted down.

Sadie poured two cups of tea, and they sat side by side on the sofa. "Nathan particularly admired your mother," Cousin Sadie said. "He often said he wished I had known her. I wish it too. She must have been an unusual woman. Why do people have to die so young?"

Ellie was afraid Sadie would burst into tears again, but she kept herself in control.

As they sat talking, Ellie kept wondering how she could broach the subject of the will. Cousin Sadie did practically all of the talking, as if she couldn't stop and speaking about her husband was an outlet for her grief. Ellie merely nodded her head.

"And what about you?" Sadie finally turned on her, looking apologetic for having gone on about herself so much. "I hear from Lena that you and Uncle Abe are not having an easy time."

This was the moment, Ellie thought, the time to speak up. But the words did not come. With a smoothness she didn't know she had, she said with a little laugh, "We're surviving. We'll be all right."

Sadie glanced at Ellie's clothes. "It would be nice," she said shyly, "and I hope you won't feel insulted, but it would be fun to take you shopping one day soon. I'd love it," she added hastily. "It would give me pleasure."

Ellie wasn't sure whether she should laugh or cry. Her hesitation lasted perhaps less than a second before she answered, "That would be nice. I wouldn't be insulted."

When she got up to leave she kissed Sadie good-bye. She nodded solemnly to Sadie's suggestion that she would call soon to make a date to go shopping.

Waiting for the elevator, Ellie was tempted for a minute to ring the apartment bell again and go back to say what she had come for. But she knew that she would not. She decided that she was about the dumbest person in the world. A real dope, she thought, a nothing who couldn't stand up for her rights, who let people walk over her. Why did she have to put on a front for Cousin Sadie? Her mother would have spoken up, would have known how to handle herself.

Out of doors the cold air hit her, and she could feel the wind whipping around her legs. She didn't feel like going home; she was too confused. Instead, she walked over to Fifth Avenue and got on a bus to go downtown. Aunt Inez was the one she wanted to talk to. She could tell Inez what a *shlemiel* she was. Perhaps Aunt Inez could console her, although Inez had been very angry when Ellie had told her about the will. "Nathan did a terrible thing," she said. "All that money. You and your father could be living on easy street. . . ."

As she expected, Ellie found her aunt Inez in the kitchen of the Italian restaurant she and her husband owned and ran. "Authentic Italian cooking in the heart of Little Italy," their advertisement read, and the restaurant on Mulberry Street had a good reputation.

"Ellie, you look so cold. Have some hot soup." Aunt Inez hugged Ellie and without waiting for an answer ladled out a plate of soup for her.

Ellie sat down at a table and sprinkled cheese over the soup. "You're busy. I shouldn't be interrupting you."

"Ach, no. I've got plenty of time. Not yet four o'clock. No one comes for a few hours yet. What's the matter? You don't look so good."

"I'm not so good. I feel terrible."

"You decide anything about the money? That's what's bothering you."

"It's more than the money. I'm such a dope, such a *shlemiel*. You can't imagine how stupid I feel." Ellie told her aunt about her visit to Cousin Sadie. "Can you imagine?" she ended up. "I sat there like a nitwit and didn't open my mouth about the will. I should have gone right back. I thought about it, but I didn't. But I will. I'll get up my courage and do it."

Her aunt was looking at her thoughtfully. "I don't think so. I've been thinking about that will, too. The money's gone, Ellie. Who knows? If your father had gotten it, it might be gone now anyway. He could have made bad investments. What's past is past. It was a mistake, but everyone makes mistakes."

Ellie was shocked. "You were the one who was so angry about it. Anyway, it's not just the money. It's my mother's whole life, what she worked for. It's as if her whole life was wasted, thrown away for nothing. When I see the way my father is living now, for no good reason. . . ." Ellie couldn't speak anymore. She was too upset.

Her aunt's dark eyes were intent. "Never say that, Ellie. Never say your mother's life was wasted. Why do you think you didn't say anything to Sadie? I'll tell you. Because you're proud. None of it was her fault. You knew that, and you didn't want any favors. You've got your mother's blood, her blood and my mother's too, and you can't get anything better. I say forget the money. Your mother didn't work just for money. Work was her life. She loved it. Sure she enjoyed what money could buy, that house in Far Rockaway, her home, her victrola, nice linens, silver. . . . I'm proud of you, Ellie. Proud you decided what you did, not to make trouble in the family for an old will. Your mother would be proud, too."

"I didn't really decide," Ellie said sheepishly. "It just happened. It makes me feel foolish."

"Don't feel foolish. You should feel good. You got

more from your mother than money, believe me. Your mother used to worry you would grow up spoiled because you had everything—the piano lessons, dancing, horseback riding, nice dresses, new shoes. Many times I told her not to worry. We all want good things for our children, the best, but Jewish women like us, who came to this country and had to work for everything, we give our children more. They say a Jewish mother is good just to make chicken soup, but that's a big lie. Our children are not stupid; they have eyes that can see. If they look they see that for everything we worked and worked hard. They can do the same. You know what I'm saying, Ellie? Your mother left you more than money, and what you have no one can take away. Not a million lawyers can touch. Be proud of yourself, Ellie. You're richer than some of the fancy girls from your college."

Ellie sat without moving, listening to her aunt. She didn't say anything.

"What's the matter? Did I hurt your feelings?" Inez asked anxiously. "Eat your soup before it gets cold."

Ellie smiled. "You're a Jewish mother after all."

Inez laughed. "All mothers tell their children to eat. But you know what I'm talking about? I want you to understand how it is." She was studying Ellie's face.

"I understand, I think." Ellie looked up and met her aunt's eyes. "It's a lot to live up to. I'm not strong like my mother, like all of you were. I *was* brought up differently. Maybe I am spoiled. I don't like being poor. In the beginning I didn't mind so much. I thought it wouldn't last. But now every day I get discouraged. The idea of getting some money was so nice."

"And when you had spent that money, then what?

You want someone always to take care of you? I don't think so. You're too smart for that. You'll be all right. Don't forget, you've got good blood in your veins."

"I hope you're right," Ellie said, and gave her aunt a hug. "I have to go. Papa will be worried about me."

When Ellie got out of the subway station uptown, the wind was still blowing, and she held her coat close around her. Before she went to the hotel, she stopped at the corner stationery store.

"Mr. Rabinowitz," she said, "remember that paper you read that I got from my cousin Nathan Solomon's estate?"

"I remember. Sure."

"I've decided to sign it. Would you notarize it for me, please."

Mr. Rabinowitz looked at her with his pale eyes. "You must be rich to sign away a lot of money."

Ellie laughed. "I am. I'm very rich."

The old man laughed with her. He doesn't know, Ellie thought, that for me it's not entirely a joke.

Outside, she dropped the stamped envelope in a mailbox and was surprised at the sense of relief she felt. As if, instead of having just lost an inheritance, she had received an unexpected gift.

About the Author

Hila Colman was born and grew up in New York City, where she went to Calhoun School. After graduation, she attended Radcliffe College. Before she started writing for herself, she wrote publicity material and ran a book club. Her first story was sold to the *Saturday Evening Post,* and since then her stories and articles have appeared in many periodicals. Some have been dramatized for television. In 1957 she turned to writing books for teen-age girls. One of them, *The Girl From Puerto Rico,* was given a special citation by the Child Study Association of America.

Mrs. Colman lives in Bridgewater, Connecticut, and has two sons.

Temple Israel

Minneapolis, Minnesota

In Honor of the Bar Mitzvah of
JEFFREY MALMON
by His Parents
Mr. & Mrs. Al Malmon

December 30, 1978